SELMA LAGERLÖF (1858-1940) was born on a farm in
Värmland, trained as a teacher and became, in her lifetime,
Sweden's most widely translated author ever. Novels such as
Gösta Berlings saga (1891; *Gösta Berling's Saga*) and *Jerusalem*
(1901-02) helped regenerate Swedish literature, and the school
reader, *Nils Holgersson's Wonderful Journey through Sweden*
(1906-07), has achieved enduring international fame and
popularity. Two very different trilogies, the Löwensköld trilogy
(1925-28) and the Mårbacka trilogy (1922-32), the latter often
taken to be autobiographical, give some idea of the range
and power of Lagerlöf's writing. Several of her texts inspired
innovative films, among them *Herr Arnes pengar* (*Sir Arne's
Treasure*), directed by Mauritz Stiller (1919) and based on *Herr
Arnes penningar* (1903; *Lord Arne's Silver*), and *Körkarlen* (*The
Phantom Carriage*), directed by Victor Sjöström (1921) and
based on Lagerlöf's *Körkarlen* (1912). She was awarded the
Nobel Prize for Literature, as the first woman ever, in 1909,
and elected to the Swedish Academy, again as the first woman,
in 1914. Having been able to buy back the farm of Mårbacka,
which her family had lost as the result of bankruptcy, Lagerlöf
spent the last three decades of her life combining her writing
with the responsibilities for running a sizeable estate. Her work
has been translated into close to 50 languages.

SARAH DEATH has been a literary translator from Swedish for over thirty-five years and has worked on books from a wide variety of genres and periods, winning various translation prizes. She has translated several titles for Norvik's 'Lagerlöf in English' series.

PETER GRAVES taught Swedish at the Universities of Aberdeen and Edinburgh. He has translated a variety of genres, particularly literature and history, and he has been awarded a number of translation prizes.

LINDA SCHENCK grew up in the United States and has lived in Sweden since she was a young adult. Her professional life has been devoted to translation and interpretation. In 2018 she was awarded the Swedish Academy Prize for translation of Swedish literature.

Some other books from Norvik Press

Victoria Benedictsson: *Money* (translated by Sarah Death)

Fredrika Bremer: *The Colonel's Family* (translated by Sarah Death)

Camilla Collett: *The District Governor's Daughters* (translated by Kirsten Seaver)

Kerstin Ekman: *Witches' Rings* (translated by Linda Schenck)
Kerstin Ekman: *The Spring* (translated by Linda Schenck)
Kerstin Ekman: *The Angel House* (translated by Sarah Death)
Kerstin Ekman: *City of Light* (translated by Linda Schenck)

The Löwensköld Trilogy
Selma Lagerlöf: *The Löwensköld Ring* (translated by Linda Schenck)
Selma Lagerlöf: *Charlotte Löwensköld* (translated by Linda Schenck)
Selma Lagerlöf: *Anna Svärd* (translated by Linda Schenck)

Selma Lagerlöf: *Lord Arne's Silver* (translated by Sarah Death)
Selma Lagerlöf: *Nils Holgersson's Wonderful Journey through Sweden* (translated by Peter Graves)
Selma Lagerlöf: *The Phantom Carriage* (translated by Peter Graves)

Klaus Rifbjerg: *Terminal Innocence* (translated by Paul Larkin)

Amalie Skram: *Fru Inés* (translated by Katherine Hanson and Judith Messick)
Amalie Skram: *Lucie* (translated by Katherine Hanson and Judith Messick)

Edith Södergran: *The Poet Who Created Herself: Selected Letters of Edith Södergran* (translated by Silvester Mazzarella)

Kirsten Thorup: *The God of Chance* (translated by Janet Garton)

Elin Wägner: *Penwoman* (translated by Sarah Death)

A Kaleidoscope of Stories

A Selection of Nine Stories

by

Selma Lagerlöf

Translated from the Swedish
by Sarah Death, Peter Graves and Linda Schenck

Series Preface by Helena Forsås-Scott

Introduction by Bjarne Thorup Thomsen

Norvik Press
2025

Originally published as: 'Mamsell Fredrika' and 'De fågelfrie' in *Osynliga länkar*, 1894; 'Gudsfreden' in *Drottningar i Kungahälla*, 1899; 'Spelmannen' and 'Silvergruvan' in *En saga om en saga och andra sagor*, 1908; 'Två spådomar', 'Bortbytingen', 'Den heliga bilden i Lucca' and 'Dimman' in *Troll och människor*, 1915.

Norvik Press Series B: English Translations of Scandinavian Literature, no. 87.

A catalogue record for this book is available from the British Library.

ISBN: 978-1-909408-73-9

Norvik Press gratefully acknowledges the generous support of Anglo-Swedish Literary Foundation towards the publication of this translation.

Norvik Press
Department of Scandinavian Studies
UCL
Gower Street
London WC1E 6BT
United Kingdom
Website: www.norvikpress.com
E-mail address: norvik.press@ucl.ac.uk

Managing editors: Elettra Carbone, Sarah Death, Janet Garton, C. Claire Thomson.

Cover design and layout: Essi Viitanen and Elettra Carbone
Cover image: Dahlia georgina from *Flora and Thalia; or, Gems of flowers and poetry: being an alphabetical arrangement of flowers, with appropriate poetical illustrations, embellished with coloured plates* (1836).

Contents

A Kaleidoscope of Stories

Women, Work and Writing

Landscapes, Families and 'Others'

Epochs, Societies and Values

An asterisk in the text indicates an Endnote. Endnotes are found at the end of each story.

Series Editor's Preface

In the first comprehensive biography of the Swedish author Selma Lagerlöf (1858-1940), Elin Wägner has provided a snapshot of her at the age of 75 that gives some idea of the range of her achievements and duties. Sitting at her desk in the library at Mårbacka with its collection of classics from Homer to Ibsen, Lagerlöf is also able to view several shelves of translations of her books. Behind her she has not only her own works and studies of herself but also a number of wooden trays into which her mail is sorted. And the trays have labels like 'Baltic Countries, Belgium, Holland, Denmark, Norway, England, France, Italy, Finland, Germany, Sweden, Switzerland, the Slavic Countries, Austria-Hungary, Bonnier [her Swedish publisher], Langen [her German publisher], Swedish Academy, the Press, Relatives and Friends, Treasures, Mårbacka Oatmeal, Miscellaneous Duties'. Lagerlöf's statement, made to her biographer Elin Wägner a few years previously, that she had at least contributed to attracting tourists to her native province of Värmland, was clearly made tongue in cheek.

How could Selma Lagerlöf, a woman born into a middle-class family in provincial Sweden around the middle of the nineteenth century, produce such an *œuvre* (sixteen novels, seven volumes of short stories) and achieve such status and fame in her lifetime?

Growing up on Mårbacka, a farm in the province of Värmland, at a time when the Swedish economy was predominantly agricultural, Selma Lagerlöf and her sisters learnt about the tasks necessary to keep the self-sufficient household ticking over, but their opportunities of getting an education beyond that which could be provided by their governess were close to non-existent. Selma Lagerlöf succeeded in borrowing money to spend three years in Stockholm training to become a teacher, one of the few professions open to women at the time, and after qualifying in 1885 she spent ten years teaching at a junior high school for girls in Landskrona, in the south of Sweden. Mårbacka had to be sold at auction in 1888, and Lagerlöf only resigned from her teaching post four years after the publication of her first novel, establishing herself as a writer in a Sweden quite different from the one in which she had grown up. Industrialisation in Sweden was late but swift, and Lagerlöf's texts found new readers among the urban working class.

Lagerlöf remained a prolific author well into the 1930s, publishing chiefly novels and short stories as well as a textbook for school children, and she soon also gained recognition in the form of honours and prizes: an Honorary Doctorate at the University of Uppsala in 1907, the Nobel Prize for Literature, as the first woman, in 1909, and election to the Swedish Academy, again as the first woman, in 1914. Suffrage for women was only introduced in Sweden in 1919, and Lagerlöf became a considerable asset to the campaign. She was also able to repurchase Mårbacka, including the farm land, and from 1910 onwards she combined her work as a writer with responsibility for a sizeable estate with a considerable number of employees.

To quote Lagerlöf's biographer, Vivi Edström, she 'knew how to tell a story without ruining it'; but her innovative literary language with its close affinity with spoken language required hard work and much experimentation. 'We authors', Lagerlöf wrote in a letter in 1908, 'regard a book as close to completion once we have found the style in which it allows itself to be written'.

Her first novel, *Gösta Berlings saga* (1891; *Gösta Berling's Saga*), was indeed a long time in the making as Lagerlöf experimented with genres and styles before settling for an exuberant and innovative form of prose fiction that is richly intertextual and frequently addresses the reader. Set in Värmland in the 1820s with the young and talented Gösta

Berling as the hero, the narrative celebrates the parties, balls and romantic adventures throughout 'the year of the cavaliers' at the iron foundry of Ekeby. But it does so against the backdrop of the expulsion of the Major's Wife who has been benefactress of the cavaliers; and following her year-long pilgrimage and what has effectively been a year of misrule by the cavaliers, it is hard work and communal responsibility that emerge as the foundations of the future.

In *Drottningar i Kungahälla* (1899; *The Queens of Kungahälla*) Lagerlöf brought together a series of short stories and an epic poem set in Viking-age Kungälv, some distance north of Gothenburg, her aim being to explore some of the material covered by the medieval Icelandic author Snorri Sturluson in *Heimskringla*, but from the perspectives of the female characters. The terse narrative of *Herr Arnes penningar* (1903; *Lord Arne's Silver*), set in the sixteenth century in a context that reinforces boundary crossings and ambivalences, has a plot revolving around murder and robbery, ghosts, love and eventual punishment. The slightly earlier short novel *En herrgårdssägen* (1899; *The Tale of a Manor*) similarly transcends boundaries as it explores music and dreams, madness and sanity, death and life in the context of the emerging relationship between a young woman and man.

A few lines in a newspaper inspired Lagerlöf to her biggest literary project since *Gösta Berling's Saga*, the two-volume novel *Jerusalem* (1901-02), which also helped pave the way for her Nobel Prize later in the decade. The plot launches straight into the topic of emigration, prominent in Sweden since the 1860s, by exploring a farming community in the province of Dalarna and the emigration of part of the community to Jerusalem. The style was inspired by the medieval Icelandic sagas, but although the focus on emigration also established a thematic link with the sagas, the inversions of saga patterns such as bloody confrontations and family feuds become more prominent as the plot foregrounds peaceful achievements and international understanding. Yet this is first and foremost a narrative in which traditional structures of stability are torn apart, in which family relationships and relations between lovers are tried and often found wanting, and in which the eventual reconciliation between old and new comes at a considerable price.

Lagerlöf had been commissioned to write a school textbook in 1901, but it was several years before she hit on the idea of presenting the geography, economy, history and culture of the provinces of Sweden through the narrative about a young boy criss-crossing the country on the back of a goose. While working on *Nils Holgerssons underbara resa genom Sverige* (1906-07; *Nils Holgersson's Wonderful Journey Through Sweden*, vols 1-2), Lagerlöf doubted that the text would find readers outside Sweden; paradoxically, however, *Nils Holgersson* was to become her greatest international success. Once perceived as an obstacle to the ambitions to award Lagerlöf the Nobel Prize for Literature, *Nils Holgersson* is nowadays read as a complex and innovative novel.

Körkarlen (1912; *The Phantom Carriage*) grew out of a request from The National Tuberculosis Society, and what was intended as a short story soon turned into a novel. The narrative about a victim of TB, whose death on New Year's Eve destines him to drive the death cart throughout the following year and who only gains the respite to atone for his failures and omissions thanks to the affection and love of others, became the basis in 1921 for one of the best-known Swedish films of the silent era, with Victor Sjöström as the director (Sjöström also played the central character) and with ground-breaking cinematography by J. Julius (Julius Jaenzon).

The First World War was a difficult time for Lagerlöf: while many of her readers, in Sweden and abroad, were expecting powerful statements against the war, she felt that the political events were draining her creative powers. *Kejsarn av Portugallien* (1914; *The Emperor of Portugallia*) is not just a novel about the miracle of a newborn child and a father's love of his daughter; it is also a text about a fantasy world emerging in response to extreme external pressures, and about the insights and support this seemingly mad world can generate. Jan, the central character, develops for himself an outsider position similar to that occupied by Sven Elversson in Lagerlöf's more emphatically pacifist novel *Bannlyst* (1918; *Banished*), a position that allows for both critical and innovative perspectives on society.

Quite different from Lagerlöf's war-time texts, the trilogy consisting of *Löwensköldska ringen* (1925; *The Löwensköld Ring*), *Charlotte Löwensköld* (1925) and *Anna Svärd* (1928) is at once lighthearted and serious, a narrative *tour de force* playing on ambivalences and multiple interpretations to an extent that has the potential to destabilise, in retrospect, any hard and fast readings of Lagerlöf's *œuvre*. As the trilogy calls into question the ghost of the old warrior General Löwensköld and then traces the demise of Karl-Artur Ekenstedt, a promising young minister in the State Lutheran Church, while giving prominence to a series of strong and independent female characters, the texts explore and celebrate the capacity and power of narrative.

Lagerlöf wrote another trilogy late in her career, and one that has commonly been regarded as autobiographical: *Mårbacka* (1922), *Ett barns memoarer* (1930; *Memoirs of a Child*), and *Dagbok för Selma Ottilia Lovisa Lagerlöf* (1932; *The Diary of Selma Lagerlöf*). All three are told in the first person; and with their tales about the Lagerlöfs, relatives, friends, local characters and the activities that structured life at Mårbacka in the 1860s and 70s, the first two volumes can certainly be read as evoking storytelling in the family circle by the fire in the evening. The third volume, *Diary*, was initially taken to be the authentic diary of a fourteen year-old Selma Lagerlöf. Birgitta Holm's psychoanalytical study of Lagerlöf's work (1984) read the Mårbacka trilogy in innovative terms and singled out *Diary* as providing the keys to Lagerlöf's *œuvre*. Ulla-Britta Lagerroth has interpreted the trilogy as a gradual unmasking of patriarchy; but with 'Selma Lagerlöf' at its centre, this work can also be read as a wide-ranging and playful exploration of gender, writing and fame.

With the publication since the 1990s of three volumes of letters by Lagerlöf, to her friend Sophie Elkan (1994), to her mother (1998), and to her friend and assistant Valborg Olander (2006), our understanding of Lagerlöf has undoubtedly become more complex. While the focus of much of the early research on Lagerlöf's work was biographical, several Swedish studies centring on the texts were published in connection with the centenary of her birth in 1958. A new wave of Lagerlöf scholarship began to emerge in Sweden in the late 1990s, exploring areas such narrative, gender, genre, and aesthetics; and in the 1990s the translation, reception and impact of Lagerlöf's texts abroad became an increasingly important field, investigated by scholars in for example the US, the UK and Japan as well as in Sweden. Current research is expanding into the interrelations between media in Lagerlöf, performance studies, and archival studies. As yet there is no scholarly edition of Lagerlöf, but thanks to the newly established Selma Lagerlöf Archive (Selma Lagerlöf-arkivet, SLA) a scholarly edition in digitised form has tentatively begun.

By the time Lagerlöf turned 80, in 1938, she was the most widely translated Swedish writer ever, and the total number of languages into which her work has been translated is now close to 50. However, most of the translations into English were made soon after the appearance of the original Swedish texts, and unlike the original texts, translations soon become dated. Moreover, as Peter Graves has concluded in a study of Lagerlöf in Britain, Lagerlöf 'was not well-served by her translators [into English]'. In other words, the publication of high-quality new translations into English of the major works of this Swedish author of world renown is long overdue.

Helena Forsås-Scott
(Most recently updated by Norvik Press 2025)

Introduction

Selma Lagerlöf and the Short Story: A Kaleidoscope of Stories

This volume presents nine new English translations of stories by Swedish Nobel-Prize-winning author Selma Lagerlöf (1858-1940). The original publication dates of the nine narratives span a 25-year period, from 1891 to 1916. While Selma Lagerlöf may be best known today for large-scale works such as *Gösta Berlings saga* (*The Saga of Gösta Berling*, 1891), *Jerusalem* (1901-02) and *Nils Holgerssons underbara resa genom Sverige* (*Nils Holgersson's Wonderful Journey through Sweden*, 1906-07), her considerable corpus of short stories and related forms of short prose is deserving of renewed attention – and up-to-date translations. Reflecting the versatility of Lagerlöf's short-prose publication practice, the stories represented here all appeared in periodical form first and book form thereafter. Measured by their first book appearance, the selected stories cover the period from 1894 to 1921.

The short story played a prominent role in Lagerlöf's writing career and reception. She experienced her first widespread critical acclaim in her capacity not as a novelist but as a short-story writer, with the collection *Osynliga länkar* (*Invisible Links*) in 1894. This was the first work by Lagerlöf to be published by Albert Bonnier, Sweden's leading publishing house. The collection was praised for its pluralism. It fitted well into a new cultural paradigm that sought to distance itself from the dominant norm of realism in order to accommodate symbolism, fantasy and the art of imagination.[i] A fusion of fantasy and realism remained a feature of Lagerlöf's writing as manifested also in subsequent short-story collections. These include *Drottningar i Kungahälla jämte andra berättelser* (*Queens of Kungahälla and Other Stories*, 1899), *En saga om en saga och andra sagor* (*The Story of a Story and Other Stories*, 1908), *Troll och människor* (*Trolls and Humans*, 1915) and *Troll och människor. Andra samlingen* (*Trolls and Humans*, Volume II, 1921). The present volume contains material from all of the above collections. The last short-prose book by Lagerlöf published in the author's own lifetime was *Höst* (*Autumn*) from 1933. Additional stories that had not previously appeared in book form were included in the posthumous collections *Från skilda tider* (*From Different Periods*), I and II (1943 and 1945). Today, several of Lagerlöf's collections may be regarded as milestones in the history of the Swedish short story. They constitute main works in their own right in the author's *oeuvre*. At the same time, the stories they contain may interface in interesting ways with her novels.

The short-prose format functioned for Lagerlöf as a fertile field for literary experimentation and diversity. The hybridity of Lagerlöf's corpus of stories and the collections in which the stories appear is striking. Consequently, this volume has been designed in order to offer the reader a multifaceted mixture of stories. The selected narratives exhibit a variety of times, places, atmospheres, styles and genre modes. Some stories are obvious instances of prose fiction, while others are balanced somewhere between fictional and factual writing. With the nine narratives listed chronologically according to their dates of first publication, the content of the volume can be showcased as follows:

* 'Mamsell Fredrika' / 'Miss Fredrika' – an imaginative and extravagantly expressed tribute to a female trailblazer in Swedish literature, centred, like many of Lagerlöf's stories, around Christmas.

* 'De fågelfrie' / 'The Outlaws' – a narrative, steeped in nature mysticism and *fin-de-siècle* feel, about clashes, but also fluid boundaries, between pagan and Christian mindsets in medieval times, fuelled by the descriptive energy that Lagerlöf attributed to her writing at the time.

* 'Gudsfreden' / 'God's Peace at Christmas' – an enquiry into a close encounter, with elements of crime, between human and animal, and Lagerlöf's first depiction of the Ingmarssons, the powerful family of peasants that would take centre stage in *Jerusalem*.

* 'Spelmannen' / 'The Fiddler' – a story, both playful and uncanny, about a self-assured musician and the shadows of abandoned family, set during a Nordic summer night in a landscape that is both attraction and trap.

* 'Silvergruvan' / 'The Silver Mine' – a nation-orientated narrative about the homeland's real riches, anticipating some of the major themes in *Nils Holgersson*.

* 'Två spådomar' / 'Two Prophecies' – a biographical sketch in six life moments, infused with motifs of deciphering, reading and writing, about Lagerlöf's road to becoming an author, published at a time when her national, and indeed international, fame was growing fast.

* 'Bortbytingen' / 'The Changeling' – a suspense-filled story about unexpected contact and strange parallels between a human and an 'alien' sphere, featuring an unconventional and resourceful heroine.

* 'Den heliga bilden i Lucca' / 'The Sacred Image in Lucca' – a miraculous *legend* and picaresque travel adventure played out in Italy, foregrounding poor but hopeful working-class characters and told in a lucid style and light-hearted tone.

* And finally 'Dimman' / 'The Mist' – a modern parable with a punishing ending, published in First World War context and critiquing attitudes, including artistic ones, to the reality of global conflict and suffering.

It is hoped that these stories, either individually or interconnected to give shape to a literary 'kaleidoscope', will make for an exciting and thought-provoking reading experience, rich in current relevance.

Supplying stories to a strong literary market

In spreading her stories, Selma Lagerlöf made maximum use of many of the publication channels on offer. With ideal timing in terms of furthering her writerly career, a new literary marketplace had developed in Sweden from the late 1880s onwards in the form of a rapidly expanding offering of illustrated cultural journals, family weeklies and Christmas annuals for adults as well as children. These outlets could attract sizeable readerships. Their editors would commission literary contributions and pay handsomely for new short-prose pieces by the most talked-about writers of the time. Periodicals of these categories in the Swedish cultural landscape during Lagerlöf's working life include: *Idun*, *Dagny*, *Nornan*, *Svea. Folk-kalender*, *Svensk Tidskrift*, *Bonniers Månadshäften*, *Ord och Bild* and a number of Christmas publications such as *Julqvällen*, *Julrosor* and *Jultomten*. A range of daily newspapers provided additional publication possibilities that Lagerlöf would use more occasionally.

Statements in Lagerlöf's correspondence at different points in her career suggest that fees from story publication in periodicals remained a not insignificant source of income for her. That such fees would have been essential in early career is perhaps not surprising. In a letter from 1894 to Swedish author Verner von Heidenstam, Lagerlöf contends in unequivocal terms that publishing short stories in Christmas magazines represents 'enda sättet att skaffa pengar' ('the only way to make some money', Toijer-Nilsson 1967, 147).[ii] At the same time, she expresses a degree of ambivalence towards the medium of the Christmas periodical, which she sees as a competitor to the book market. In another letter from the same year, to Danish-Swedish author Helena Nyblom, Lagerlöf's ambivalence towards publication in periodicals seems to concern a perceived lack of literary prestige and prominence: 'Och så mycket värde jag annars sätter på noveller, så synes det mig, att de ta sig så litet ut i jultidningar' ('And although I set great store by short stories, they do seem to make only a very small splash in Christmas magazines', Toijer-Nilsson 1967, 160). However, what is also clear from this quote is Lagerlöf's high estimation of the short story as such. Twenty years on, in 1914 at the height of her career, the periodical appears, despite the reservations, to have retained its dual importance as a disseminator of the results of Lagerlöf's short-story creativity and as an income generator. In a letter to her friend and associate Valborg Olander, Lagerlöf gives an insight into her ongoing engagement, both artistic and economic, with short-story writing:

Det hände sig år 1912, att jag skulle skriva en bit för Idun, som jag hade lovat under jubileumsåret, och jag vet inte vad som var åt mig, jag började den ena novellen efter den andra men kunde inte göra någon färdig. Dessa bitar äro inte så oävna nu, då jag läser om dem. En har jag gjort klar och två andra skall jag försöka göra i ordning för att få litet pengar, så att jag kan klara mig under denna svåra februarimånad. (Toijer-Nilsson 2006, 102-03)

(It so happened in 1912 that I was writing a piece for *Idun* as I had promised for their silver jubilee, and, well, I can't imagine what my problem was, but I started one story after the next without being able to complete any of them. Looking back at them now, these fragments aren't all that bad. I've finished one and am trying to make something of two others so as to earn a bit of money to get me through this difficult month of February.)[iii]

A closer look at the specific periodicals in which the stories selected for this volume were first published reveals considerable outlet variation as well as good matches between medium and story content. *Idun. Illustrerad tidning för kvinnan och hemmet* (*Idun. Illustrated Weekly for Women and the Home*), which Lagerlöf references in her letter, presented 'En bortbyting' ('A Changeling')[iv] in its Christmas issue in 1908. This would seem an appropriate outlet for a story that is family-orientated in a new and drastic way and has a strong and complex female dimension. *Idun* was established in 1887 and is iconic in Lagerlöf's overall publication history as the magazine whose literary prize competition she won in 1890 with extracts from *The Saga of Gösta Berling*, which kick-started her career. However, it was only after the turn of the century that *Idun* acquired its distinctive profile as a cultural weekly with a perspective on women's life *outside* the domestic sphere and as a mouthpiece for their emancipation (Nordlund 2005, 31). Other strong fits between story and periodical are shown by the early narrative 'Miss Fredrika' and the mid-career 'Two Prophecies'. 'Miss Fredrika' was published in 1891 in *Dagny. Tidskrift för sociala och litterära intressen* (*Dagny. Journal for Social and Literary Interests*). This was a pioneering feminist magazine founded in 1886 and published by the association dedicated to the great Swedish writer, traveller and social reformer Fredrika Bremer (1801-1865). The issue of *Dagny* in which Lagerlöf's appreciation of Bremer appears commemorates the 25th anniversary of her death. Equally appropriately, Lagerlöf's account in 'Two Prophecies' of her own path towards the writing profession featured in a periodical with a close connection to the institution that was the primary disseminator of her work. It appeared in 1908 in *Bonniers Månadshäften* (*Bonnier's Monthly*), the illustrated cultural magazine for a broader readership which her publishing house had established the previous year. Lagerlöf's piece, which has the subtitle 'Ett stycke lefnadsteckning' ('A Biographical Fragment'), was published at a point when her 'cultural capital' was at a high: one year after the completion of the hugely impactful *Nils Holgersson* and one year prior to the award of the Nobel Prize for Literature. The piece itself and, not least, its paratextual presentation in the periodical reflect Lagerlöf's status and a growing focus on her public persona. Lagerlöf's contribution is the headline story of the issue and is accompanied by no fewer than six portraits of the author and two further illustrations of, respectively, her birthplace at Mårbacka and her home in Falun at the time of publication. The illustrations comprise photographs and reproduced art works and are flagged up in the issue's table of contents.

Another periodical forming part of Bonnier's publishing empire, *Svea. Folk-Kalender* (*Svea. A People's Calendar*), provided the outlet for two of the stories in this volume, 'The Outlaws' and 'The Silver Mine', appearing in 1892 and 1903 respectively. *Svea*, established as early as 1844, was published yearly in time for the Christmas book trade and was the most widely circulated of Sweden's cultural annuals, so-called 'calendars' (its main competitor was *Nornan*).ᵛ *Svea*'s national framing offered an apt fit for the two narratives as they illuminate the zeitgeist and schisms in different periods of Swedish history: the Middle Ages and the late eighteenth century. 'The Fiddler' likewise belongs to the culture of annuals – and to Christmas. It was published in 1903 in the children's annual *Fågel Blå* (*Blue Bird*), which was established in 1898 as a subsidiary of a Christmas magazine for children titled *Jultomten* (*Father Christmas*). A decade later, 'The Sacred Image in Lucca' appeared in the popular Christmas magazine *Julqvällen* (*A Christmas Evening*), established in 1881.

The connection between the Christmas season and a substantial segment of Lagerlöf's stories and their publication channels is well documented and evidenced by the majority of narratives in this volume. Vivi Edström observes that a considerable number of Lagerlöf's stories belong to the national cultural heritage and that this is particularly the case for those that engage with Christmas and winter and were intended as literary entertainment for the holidays (Edström 1983, 5). The enduring popularity of this type of story is borne out by the publication in 2022 of a volume entitled *Selma Lagerlöf's jul* (Christmas with Selma Lagerlöf), appropriately containing 24 of the author's seasonal pieces. In its foreword, Anna-Karin Palm notes that the Christmas stories would traditionally be consumed by reading them aloud in a family setting. This meant that they should appeal to a broad audience, including both adults and children (Palm 2022, 8). This, in turn, would impact on style and encourage use of suspense elements and happy endings. The relevance of Lagerlöf's Christmas-related stories to a contemporary international readership is demonstrated, finally, by the publication in 2024 of a collection of eight of these stories in English translation in the Penguin Classics series. The collection is titled *A Book for Christmas*. The translators are Sarah Death, Peter Graves and Linda Schenck, whose work is also showcased in this volume.[vi]

The seasonal connection carries, furthermore, some broader significance for the interpretative approach to Lagerlöf's stories. When critically appreciating the harmonising features that they frequently display, it is important to recognise that these features may be determined, firstly, by the author's faithfulness to the uplifting seasonal role of the stories and their outlets. Secondly, they may be determined by her fidelity to the traditional – and for her readership comfortingly familiar – genre designations she regularly chooses for her stories, not least the seasonal ones (designations that were more commonly stated in the periodical version of a story than in its book version): a *saga* should end happily, while a *legend* should climax with a miracle.[vii] This does not imply, however, that Lagerlöf's stories are 'innocent' or 'harmless' writing, but rather the opposite: the stories' harmonising surfaces should be explored in an interplay – or even tension – with their deeper or contemporary meanings. Notions of traditional or harmless literature are challenged by the will to experiment that was touched upon in the previous section and by the interventionist and ideological impulse that informs Lagerlöf's story writing, as discussed in the next section.

Returning to the diversity of outlets used by Lagerlöf, daily newspapers, finally, figure as the periodical medium for two stories presented in this volume. 'God's Peace at Christmas' was published on New Year's Eve 1898 in the liberal and Lagerlöf-loyal *Göteborgs Handels- och Sjöfartstidning*, while 'The Mist' was published on 6 August 1916 in *Dagens Nyheter*, whose majority shareholder Bonnier had become in 1909. The newspaper layouts of the two stories mirror the considerable difference in Lagerlöf's public prestige at the times of publication. 'God's Peace at Christmas' occupies a fairly inconspicuous place on page three and four of the paper, positioned alongside small snippets of news, occasional poetry, advertisements and chess diagrams. There is no accompanying illustration and no emphasis on the identity of the author, only her name given in a small typeface. The layout of 'The

Mist', in contrast, radiates the aura of an author at the height of her fame. The story dominates the front page of the paper's Sunday magazine and continues over the bulk of page three. Its headline is printed in a large artistic typeface, and the story is illustrated with a prominent oval photograph of the author, framed and decorated in art-nouveau style.

As for the role of the book medium in disseminating Lagerlöf's short-story writing, Albert Bonnier's publishing house showed a keen interest in releasing short-story collections regularly, and particularly in years when no other book by Lagerlöf was forthcoming, in order to maintain publishing momentum and public interest in one of their bestselling assets. Far from all of Lagerlöf's stories, however, undertook the journey from periodical to book format,[viii] and when it happened, the journey time could amount to several years. Conversely, a small proportion of stories would be written directly for the collections. Certain stories would be published in multiple print versions, with 'The Mist' a case in point.[ix] The dynamism and fluidity of the circulation patterns of Lagerlöf's story writing are thus noticeable in many publication aspects. It is evidenced also by the fact that identically titled editions of a story collection could vary in content. This is particularly the case for *Invisible Links,* whose original selection of stories from 1894 was radically changed and expanded from the 1904 third edition onwards, not least by incorporating several stories that had first appeared in *Queens of Kungahälla and Other Stories* in 1899, one of the most diverse of Lagerlöf's collections, as its somewhat cumbersome title may suggest.[x]

As mentioned, all of the stories selected for this volume were published in both periodical and book form. Measured on this limited material, the average time gap between the two modes of publication amounts to approximately four years. The stories formed part of the following collections: 'Miss Fredrika' and 'The Outlaws' were published in the original edition of *Invisible Links* and remained part of this collection also after its revision. 'God's Peace at Christmas' was originally published in *Queens of Kungahälla* but was transferred to the revised edition of *Invisible Links.* 'The Silver Mine' and 'The

Fiddler' appeared in *The Story of a Story and Other Stories* in 1908 – a collection that was riding on the wave of the success of *Nils Holgersson*, completed the previous year. Three stories, 'The Changeling', 'Two Prophecies' and 'The Sacred Image in Lucca', were published in the highly regarded *Trolls and Humans* in 1915. The latter story represented Lagerlöf's return to the religiously informed *legend* genre after a period of de-prioritising this strand of her short-prose writing (Kant 1983, 153). Its role in her *oeuvre* had culminated with the nationally and internationally hugely popular collections *Legender* (*Legends*) and *Kristuslegender* (*Legends of Christ*), both from 1904. 'The Mist', finally, was published in *Trolls and Humans*, Volume II, in 1921 – a collection that is of interest not least due to its fractured perspectives on the First World War period and the moral dilemmas it posed.

The short story as interventionist writing

While polyphony, ambiguity and interpretative openness undoubtedly form key qualities of Lagerlöf's short prose, most of the stories contained in this volume may at the same time be characterised as value-based writing in various ways. Alongside its experimental function, the short-prose format provided Lagerlöf with a usefully confined canvas for ideological scrutiny and ethical messaging. One of Lagerlöf's main authorial roles is as an interventionist writer who wishes to influence her readers and the surrounding society. In Lagerlöf's story world, lines of enquiry that are topical or controversial can frequently be dressed or 'masked' in traditional form, as commented on above, while other stories are more overtly modern. This final section will suggest a few value-focused pairings of or connections between selected stories – not to the exclusion of a raft of other readings, of course.

A pairing along gender-ideological lines may be formed by the (auto)biographically inspired stories 'Miss Fredrika' and 'Two Prophecies'. In the former piece, a wider aspect of its appreciation of Fredrika Bremer is the celebration of the significant cultural and societal contributions made by unmarried women. The story draws attention to the predicament and marginalisation of this group of women in traditional society – which Bremer sought to counteract – as well as welcoming the changing role and status of single women in modern society. In the discussion of the story in her 1942 Lagerlöf biography, journalist and novelist Elin Wägner characterises Bremer as 'de ogifta kvinnornas vapendragare' ('the champion of unmarried women') and emphasises the struggle for their 'rätt till yrkesutbildning' ('right to education in the professions', Wägner 1942, 154) as a theme in 'Miss Fredrika'. Years later, echoes of this theme can be found in Lagerlöf's take on her own trajectory towards independence in 'Two Prophecies'. This is especially the case in its fifth episode. This conveys, in the present-tense register that contributes immediacy throughout the narrative, the protagonist's anxiety and sense of being at a crossroads in life as she awaits the outcome of her entry exam into the Stockholm Teacher Training College for Women. If she passes, a liberating career path, as well as a knowledge platform for becoming an author, will open up for her. If she fails, she will be drawn back into dependency and prejudice in her first family. In this volume, 'Two Prophecies' and 'Miss Fredrika' together constitute the first of three thematic sections of stories under the heading of *Women, Work and Writing*. 'Two Prophecies' has been chosen as the front piece of the collection overall since it provides a portal to Lagerlof's progression towards a literary career.

Another pairing of stories can be formed by 'God's Peace at Christmas' and 'The Changeling'. When viewed through an ethical lens, these tales come together as critiques of anthropocentric behaviour and privilege. Their moral intent may be found in the argument that the welfare of the human being is co-dependent on the welfare of the 'other' being, be it animal or 'troll'. This is a message of compassion, tolerance and peace that has far-reaching applications – ecological, geopolitical, racial and gendered, to name some. It is connected to Lagerlöf's recurring interest in the domains that lie beyond the confines of what is defined as the 'real' or the 'central'. If violence and weaponry are the responses to these domains and their inhabitants, the consequences are dire, as both tales demonstrate. However, both tales equally display the life-sustaining potential of 'cross-border' contact and respect – an insight notably associated with female characters in both cases.[xi] Together with 'The Fiddler', which, too, displays liminal characters and zones as well as an interest in reconciliation, 'God's Peace at Christmas' and 'The Changeling' constitute the volume's second thematic section of stories under the heading of *Landscapes, Families and 'Others'*.

As for the promotion of national value in Lagerlöf's writing, 'The Silver Mine' is a case in point. The story is played out in the province of Dalarna, which traditionally carries Swedish national symbolism and forms the core setting of the first volume of *Jerusalem*, published two years previously. The story explores how the discovery of a rich seam of silver ore leads to the moral contamination of a community. 'The Silver Mine' goes on to argue, endorsed by no less than the monarch, that the populace – rather than metals – are the nation's most precious resource. This would chime with the strong presence and valorisation of the national 'flock' in *Nils Holgersson*, the planning of which would have been ongoing at the time of the publication of the story. 'The Silver Mine' may fruitfully be read alongside 'The Sacred Image in Lucca'. This, too, takes place in a national terrain of sorts, which its bold protagonists – representatives of the ordinary people – traverse in search of monetary and spiritual value. Their mobile mission and the miracle it effects connects space and people, and the narrative displays elements of a wonderful journey.

'The Silver Mine' and 'The Sacred Image in Lucca' are joined by 'The Outlaws' and 'The Mist' to form the volume's third and final thematic section of stories under the heading of *Epochs, Societies and Values*. The section spans from the medieval to the modern and from the national to the global. 'The Outlaws' explores the ambivalence of values in an epoch that is transitioning from one belief system to another. The story complicates concepts such as crime, retribution and justice – as well as emotional bonds – through its depiction of the relationship between two men outlawed from a medieval society. Moving into the contemporary epoch, it is evident, finally, that Lagerlöf's interventionist impulse was particularly urgent during the First World War. This is illustrated by her anti-war novel *Bannlyst* (*Banished*, 1918) and by a range of short prose that shows intense involvement with the burning questions of the time in experimental and fragmented forms. A group of these prose pieces, including 'The Mist', was published in *Trolls and Humans*, Volume II, under the umbrella name of 'Stämningar från krigsåren' ('The Mood of the War Years').[xii] 'The Mist' debates and ultimately dismisses as morally corrupt the attractions of self-sufficiency and isolationism – encapsulated in the titular motif – at a time of world crisis. While a shortened field of vision may be mentally soothing and artistically pleasing, the narrative reveals it as a false value. Instead, it advocates global responsibility. 'The Mist' thus demonstrates the maximum reach of Lagerlöf's many-sided engagement with moral and ideological questions in her rich body of short stories.

Finally, it should be noted that the stories presented in the following display US spelling when translated by Linda Schenck and UK spelling when translated by Sarah Death and Peter Graves. Swedish-language versions of the stories are available online from Litteraturbanken: https://litteraturbanken.se/

Endnotes

[i] For the reception history of *Invisible Links* and for the new cultural paradigm, see Nordlund 2005, 71-74.

[ii] The dependency on fees and royalties would become particularly pronounced after 1895, when Lagerlöf left her position as a teacher to become a full-time writer.

[iii] For further perspectives on Lagerlöf's statements about her short-story writing and the short-story genre, see Ritte 1983, 135-40.

[iv] The title of the story was changed from the indefinite to the definite form, 'Bortbytingen', when the story was published in book form in 1915 (see below).

[v] In the Swedish cultural landscape, the 'calendar' represented a particular type of annual publication that offered its readership a varied mixture of material, which could include lists of Swedish and international royalty, short stories and poems by the nation's foremost authors, travelogues, essays and obituaries. The format of this type of annual featured numerous illustrations, frequently including reproductions of works by contemporary Swedish artists.

[vi] Interestingly, the titular story of this collection, a memory piece first published in 1933, takes as its topic precisely the connection between Christmas and the supply of reading matter. The main storyline concerns the young first-person protagonist's prolonged state of being on tenterhooks during the distribution of presents on Christmas Eve, waiting, with fading hope, for the only type of present that truly matters to her – a book. During the wait, in a subsidiary episode, her aunt is given a novel as well as copies of both *Svea* and *Nornan*, exemplifying the culture of annuals discussed above.

[vii] In contrast, a *sägen* should end in a tragic or catastrophic way, a prime example being 'Gammal fäbodsägen' ('A Traditional Summer Pasture Tale'), first published in 1914.

[viii] For perspectives on Lagerlöf's lesser-known short prose, including pieces which remained unpublished, see Thomsen 2013 and Thomsen 2014.

[ix] In addition to its newspaper version discussed above and its later inclusion in a story collection as mentioned below, 'The Mist' interestingly also appeared independently in 1916 as a four-page folio published by Svenska Andelsförlaget in Stockholm. The layout of this publication is striking, with each page featuring decorative borders displaying skulls, bones and crosses as a strong reminder of the war-time context. In the same year, furthermore, 'The Mist' appeared in the anthology *En rättfärdig fred. Tankar och opinionsyttringar* (A Just Peace. Thoughts and Opinion Pieces), published by Neutrala Konferensen in Stockholm.

[x] The collection combined a cycle of narratives (originally written in poetical form) about medieval queens in western Sweden, a group of legends with biblical motifs and a section of more 'standard' short stories. It was the latter that was later amalgamated into *Invisible Links*. Lagerlöf herself characterised *Queens of Kungahälla and Other Stories* as unmanageable (Edström 2002, 232).

[xi] Vivi Edström identifies the confrontation between female and male positions as a theme in 'God's Peace at Christmas' and observes that the theme would resurface in *Jerusalem* (Edström 2002, 239-41). It is found in 'The Changeling' too, it could be added.

[xii] For further discussion of 'The Mood of the War Years' and Lagerlöf's creative vision during the war period, see Thomsen 2014, 198-202.

Works cited

Edström, Vivi. 1983. 'Inledning.' *Lagerlöfstudier. Om Selma Lagerlöfs noveller*: 5-6.

Edström. Vivi. 2002. *Selma Lagerlöf. Livets vågspel.* Stockholm: Bokförlaget Natur och Kultur.

Kant, Yngve. 1983. 'Selma Lagerlöfs noveller – en översikt.' *Lagerlöfstudier. Om Selma Lagerlöfs noveller*: 149-200.

Lagerlöf, Selma. 2024. *A Book for Christmas: And Other Stories.* Translated by Sarah Death, Peter Graves and Linda Schenck. London: Penguin Classics.

Nordlund, Anna. 2005. *Selma Lagerlöfs underbara resa genom den svenska litteraturhistorien 1891–1996.* Stockholm and Stehag: Brutus Östlings Bokförlag Symposion.

Palm, Anna-Karin. 2022. 'Förord.' In *Selma Lagerlöfs jul*, 7-12. Stockholm: Romanus & Selling.

Ritte, Hans. 1983. 'Selma Lagerlöf och novellen. Om några problem kring genrebeteckningen.' *Lagerlöfstudier. Om Selma Lagerlöfs noveller*: 135-47.

Thomsen, Bjarne Thorup. 2013. 'Text, Traffic and Transnational Thought. Perspectives on prose publications by Selma Lagerlöf in periodicals and anthologies, with particular reference to "En emigrant" (1914), "Lappland-Schonen" (1917) and the First World War period.' *Scandinavica. An International Journal of Scandinavian Studies*: 208-24.

Thomsen, Bjarne Thorup. 2014. 'Text and transnational terrain.' In *Re-Mapping Lagerlöf. Performance, Intermediality, and European Transmissions*, edited by Helena Forsås-Scott, Lisbeth Stenberg and Bjarne Thorup Thomsen, 187-206. Lund: Nordic Academic Press.

Toijer-Nilsson, Ying, ed. 1967. *Selma Lagerlöf. Brev*, vol. 1, *1871-1902.* Lund: Gleerups Förlag.

Toijer-Nilsson, Ying, ed. 2006. *En riktig författarhustru. Selma Lagerlöf skriver till Valborg Olander.* Stockholm: Albert Bonniers Förlag.

Wägner, Elin. 1942. *Selma Lagerlöf*, vol. I, *Från Mårbacka till Jerusalem.* Stockholm: Albert Bonniers Förlag.

Women, Work and Writing

TWO PROPHECIES

Två spådomar*

Translated by Sarah Death

It is easy to imagine all the fuss and bother there must have been at the old Mårbacka farmhouse on the twentieth of November 1858. A child was born there, quite late in the evening, and that sort of thing always involves commotion and anxiety even in a place where they are in the habit of taking things calmly and not making more ado about anything than it frankly deserves.

In the dark of night, towards nine o'clock, the vicar's wife, who lives at the property next door, comes over and pokes her head around the kitchen door. She is a little old lady, a relative and a good friend, known to everyone as Aunt Wennervik. She simply could not still her impatience at home any longer but threw a shawl over her head, took up a lantern and made her way along the little shortcut that runs behind the garden, to hear how things were going.

The vicar's wife is immediately shown into the bedroom off the kitchen. To this day, it is the domain of old Mrs Lagerlöf, widow of Regimental Paymaster Lagerlöf, and it is a room in which she has lived her whole life, as a married woman and as a young girl. Now seventy and white-haired, she is seated at one end of her sofa knitting socks for her grandchildren, as always. In her room things are always calm, and she herself is serenity personified because her son, who has taken over the house and farm after his father, has just been in to tell her that the worst is over and the child has been brought into the world.

Late in the day though it is, the housekeeper puts the coffee pan on the stove and before long she comes in with a fully laid coffee tray. Then Aunt Wennervik and old Mrs Lagerlöf drink coffee, all by themselves. Aunt Wennervik receives the news that the new baby is a daughter and the two elderly ladies, who are nearing the limit of their lifespans, sit and chat about what sort of life this little girl might lead.

'She will lead the life she is worthy of, no more and no less,' says old Mrs Lagerlöf.

'But let me tell you, sister, it is all a matter of chance, too,' replies Aunt Wennervik.

As the vicar's wife makes this remark, old Mrs Lagerlöf leans forward and feels the cloth bag that Aunt Wennervik always carries on her arm. It contains a thousand things, for Aunt Wennervik is the kind of person who can solve any problem, and she must therefore be prepared for people to come and ask her for help. She is Mrs Lagerlöf's sister-in-law and was a woman of mature years when she married Pastor Wennervik, who is Mrs Lagerlöf's brother; before that she was housekeeper at many large estates. That is why she knows how to do everything, from preparing a wedding feast and threading a loom for the finest twill to curing the sick and preparing young farmers' daughters to be good homemakers.

When Mrs Lagerlöf feels the cloth bag, she soon discovers that besides the spectacles and the bunch of keys and the sewing kit and the cough lozenges and the medicine bottle and the book of weaving patterns and the smelling salts there is also a hard, rectangular object.

'I can feel that you have brought your cards with you,' she says.

Aunt Wennervik's wizened cheeks flush a little. She can tell fortunes, and she never does a card reading without everything she predicts coming to pass. She has something of a weakness for being called upon to demonstrate her abilities, though she tries to pretend otherwise. She declares that she did not have the faintest idea she had brought the cards with her. She simply cannot fathom how they found their way into her bag.

'But seeing as they happen to be there, sister, you may as well read the cards for this poor little scrap who has just come into the world,' says old Mrs Lagerlöf.

Aunt Wennervik at first protests that she couldn't possibly, but proves easy enough to persuade, so the coffee tray is set aside and the elderly wife of the vicar starts laying out her cards. She handles them with such dexterity that as old Mrs Lagerlöf sits watching her, she cannot help thinking her sister-in-law looks like a proper fortune-teller.

She has a brownish complexion, dark, restless eyes and a long, aquiline nose. On her head she wears a black lace cap that comes down to a point at her forehead, and at each temple she has three corkscrew curls. She has not a single grey hair on her head, but her whole face is covered in a web of fine lines.

Aunt Wennervik lays out the cards in four rows with nine cards in each row, and once that is done, she puts her index finger on the first card and starts to count: one, two, three, four, all the way to sixteen. She counts upwards and downwards and back and forth, moving her finger as she counts, until she reaches the sixteenth card. Then she mutters under her breath, as if she is not entirely satisfied.

'Well sister, what do you see?' asks old Mrs Lagerlöf.

'There is some kind of sickliness dogging her,' replies the vicar's wife, 'and I believe she will have to contend with it all her life.'

'We each have our cross to bear, otherwise we would never turn into mature people,' says old Mrs Lagerlöf. She has a positive outlook and always sees the bright side of everything. 'If she is sickly, then she will probably have to live a quiet life, and that is the best path for anyone, really.'

Aunt Wennervik plants her finger on the cards and starts counting again. 'Many a long journey lies ahead of her,' she says, giving her sister-in-law a slightly droll look. 'And she will have to move house any number of times and find new places to live.'

'A rolling stone gathers no moss,' says old Mrs Lagerlöf. Having herself lived on the same farm all her days, she is not exactly happy that her grandchild will be the sort who is forever flitting about the kingdom of Sweden. 'I can well understand, though, that if she turns out sickly, she won't be able to earn her own living but will be sent from pillar to post to stay with assorted family members. It isn't easy for a person who can't work and make herself useful.'

'She will toil and labour all her days,' declares Aunt Wennervik after another round of counting. 'You need have no fear of that, sister.'

'Oh, so I suppose that means she will have to earn her crust in the homes of others and change her master, over and over again,' says old Mrs Lagerlöf with a sigh. She has no experience of being in service anywhere, and it seems to her the worst of all fates. 'But things have gone well for you, sister,' she says, her face brightening. 'Imagine if she turns out to be as capable as you, dear!'

'Oh, she won't have to thread a loom for twill in her entire life,' says Aunt Wennervik with her nose almost in her cards, and so absorbed is she in divining what the future holds that she spares no thought for whether her prophecies are pleasing or displeasing. 'She will have a great deal to do with books and papers, sister, just you wait and see.'

Old Mrs Lagerlöf bends over the cards too, as if to find a meaning in the jumble.

'A great deal to do with books and papers?' she says quizzically. 'Perhaps you mean, dear, that she will marry a poor clergyman, who is obliged to move from parish to parish and can never settle down. But as long as he is a good man, who treats her kindly ...'

Aunt Wennervik holds one finger up in the air and interrupts her.

'Do you want me to be frank, sister?'

'I do indeed,' says old Mrs Lagerlöf.

'She will never marry.'

'Oh, so she will never marry!' says old Mrs Lagerlöf, keeping herself firmly in check so as not to show how disappointed she is. 'Well, perhaps that way she will be spared many sorrows. But surely you can at least see whether she will be a fine, good human being?'

'She will most certainly be kind-hearted and obliging,' says

Aunt Wennervik, bending over the cards again to spy out more secrets, but this time it is she who is interrupted, and old Mrs Lagerlöf says rather bluntly:

'Don't trouble yourself to say any more, sister. I am content to have learned that she will be a decent person. That really is the only thing one needs to know.'

*

There is a book called *Oceola*', although I might possibly have misremembered and it has some other splendidly exotic name. It is an adventure yarn, as they say these days, although we may be sure it was not originally written for children, but intended to be read by grown-ups, too. I do not know the name of the author, nor do I know when it was written, but it is most likely quite old, because it is over forty years since I first set eyes on it.

I cannot say how the book happened to find its way to my home up in Värmland. It did not belong in the household's own collection of books, which largely consisted of works in verse and included very few novels. It could have been that some traveller brought it with them, or perhaps my aunt, an eager consumer of novels, had borrowed it from one of the neighbours. But anyway, one fine day when I am about seven or eight years old it is most definitely lying there on a table at home, and I happen to catch sight of it.

I like reading and I generally sit on a low chair beside Mother every day as she works at her sewing and read aloud from Nösselt's *General History for Women**. We have read our way through all seven parts, but it is the first part I understand best, with all the stories. I can never help feeling pleased when Odysseus comes home and shoots the suitors dead, but I prefer to skip the parting of Hector and Andromache, because I can never read it without weeping.

Fritiof's Saga, Andersen's *Fairy Tales* and *The Tales of Ensign Stål** are among my other good friends, but this is the first time I have ever had a novel before my eyes. I have no intention of reading such a thick volume, either; it looks as though it would take years to finish, and I merely leaf through it. But as luck would have it, I happen to open the book at exactly the place where the heroine of the novel, the young and beautiful daughter of a plantation owner, is ambushed by an alligator when she goes to bathe. I read about her running away, pursued by the creature and in mortal danger. Never before have I read anything that puts me in such suspense. I stand there with my heart in my mouth and read until the young and heroic Red Indian rushes to her aid and, after a fearful struggle with the alligator, plunges his knife into its heart.

After that I read page after page, for as long as I am left in peace. And whenever I have a spare moment and do not have to sit in the schoolroom learning to write, read and do sums, I sneak off to *Oceola*, which is still where I left it, and carry on reading.

I am utterly captivated, utterly enchanted. I think about the book day and night. It is a new world that I have suddenly discovered. Here is all the rich abundance of life, revealing itself to me for the first time. Here are love, deeds of valour, beautiful and noble people, base villains, perils and delight, bliss and failure. Above all, it is an artfully interlocking series of events that generates suspense and expectation. It is every possible thing a seven-year-old child growing up on a quiet farm never dreamed might exist.

Once I have finished *Oceola*, I immerse myself in all the other novels I can find. It would be no easy matter to say how much I understand of them, but I enjoy them more than I can say. Most, however, have completely vanished from my memory.

When I think back to that time it surprises me that they let me read whatever I wanted. But I realise that Mother and Father found it hard to deny me that. The sickliness that Aunt Wennervik had prophesied for me had already manifested itself. One of my legs was weak and there were long periods when I could not walk at all. It was not considered good for me to amuse myself with outdoor games and physical exercise like the other children and it was felt preferable for me to keep still. When my parents saw that I was happy as long as I had a book in my hand, they did not want to rob me of that pleasure.

For me, the encounter with the adventure yarn *Oceola*

proves crucial to the rest of my life. It arouses in me a deep and powerful desire to create something equally wonderful. It is this book that makes me aware, even at such a young age, that what I most want to do in my allotted days is to write novels.

My siblings and nurserymaids have told me about the prophecy that old Aunt Wennervik made on the night I was born. Nobody at all is happy with it, except for me. I am content, because it predicts that I will have many dealings with books and writing. In those days, it was all I asked.

*

When I am nine years old, another of Aunt Wennervik's ill-boding prophecies comes true. I am obliged to undertake a long journey. I am sent to Stockholm to seek treatment for my bad leg, and the doctor prescribes a therapeutic course at a gymnastics institute. I stay in Stockholm all winter long and find the treatment very beneficial. When I get back home in the spring, I am as strong as other children, and my limp is barely noticeable.

I live with some close relations*, who are very good to me, but I cannot help feeling a little homesick. It is hard for me to adjust to city life. I find it bothersome that I must put on a hat and coat every time I go out, and I do not like the long, straight paved streets, where little children are expected to walk as meekly and primly as the grown-ups. And I do not understand the Stockholm children's games, either. Their toboggans feel too small to me, and I do not care for dolls at all. I feel stupid and awkward in the company of these deft and dainty youngsters and I am afraid of being laughed at, because of my Värmland accent.

But there are things in Stockholm that are beyond all description and provide compensation for any hardship. My uncle, for example, has a bookcase with a shelf containing all the novels of Walter Scott, and he lends them to me one by one, so I have a chance to read them all. And then there is the theatre!

My relations have a faithful old servant living under their

roof, who used to run my uncle's household, before he married. She is too old for domestic duties but sits at her crochet and knitting in a comfortable armchair in her own little room, day in and day out. Uncle is very good to her. He is afraid she will find life too dull and comes in quite often to slip her a theatre ticket. And when the old woman goes to the theatre, I am allowed to go with her. My relations have realised what extraordinary pleasure it gives me, and perhaps they are also a little nervous about letting the old servant go on her own. What is more, my theatre visits cost nothing. Old Ulla has only to drop a friendly word to the usher, and he lets me in. I don't get a seat, of course, and have to stand in front of her, but what does that matter? Time flies by in the theatre. I never start to feel tired before it is all over.

There are probably people around today who still remember the worn staircases and narrow passageways of the old Opera House. And probably there are still one or two who remember the special smell of the corridors. I sometimes find myself entering some theatre in a foreign country, where that special smell still lingers. And every time I catch that scent, I am filled with a blissful sense of expectation. I feel as if I am a child again, standing outside the door of our box and waiting for the usher to open it.

Ulla and I are always in the centre of the upper circle, in the front row. We don't only go to the Opera House, we also attend the Dramatic Theatre, but we have the same seat there.

Thus it is that the two of us are able to see *The African Woman*, *Robert*, *The Mute Girl*, *The Marksman*, *The Värmlanders*, *Fair Helen*, *The School for Wives*, *Hotbed Flowers* and *My Rose in the Forest*.*

Once again it is a completely new and colourful world into which I am led. You might have thought it would make me entirely giddy.

It is undeniably just as well that I have spent that time beside my mother's sewing table, reading Nösselt's *General History*, for how else could I find my way around?

But it is not really an entirely new and colourful world. Rather it is the familiar world of my novels that has come alive and is being performed for me in living pictures. So this is the way they look, my savages, my knights in armour? This is how a king is dressed, this is how a monastery is organised, and those long grey cowls are what monks and nuns wear to go about in! I can acquaint myself with stormy seas, tropical landscapes and fiery volcanoes. And naturally I take it all as entirely credible and in earnest. I do not realise that Fair Helen is one big joke. I firmly believe that this is how it happened when Helen was abducted by Prince Paris, even though Nösselt has neglected to mention it.

We have exactly the same tastes, the old lady and I. We like showy scenery, showy costumes, big scenes in which the stage is teeming with people. And our main interest is the plot, of course. We care little for the singing and music. In fact they trouble us, because we find it difficult to hear the words as they are sung and lose track of what is going on.

We are not that impressed by performances in which no kings or knights appear. For my part I am quite happy with a play about ordinary people, like *The Värmlanders*, because it reminds me of my home district. But Ulla, the old lady, does not like seeing only peasants on the stage. She hurts me deeply when she says that Fair Helen with her host of kings was something entirely different. I am offended on my fellow-countrymen's behalf, although at heart I agree with her.

Winter comes to an end, however, and when spring arrives, I am allowed back home. And naturally I carry with me the memories of everything I have seen, and tell my brothers and sisters all about it, repeatedly.

One day when for some reason we are not tied to our lessons, we have the idea of pretending to be in the theatre and putting on one of the plays I saw in Stockholm. And the one we decide to perform is *My Rose in the Forest*. Not because it was the most enjoyable of all the plays I saw, but because it is the simplest and the only one we feel capable of staging.

It proves a taxing day for me. I am the one who must work out all the parts and teach the performers their lines. We have no printed script, only my memory to rely on. I am the one who, with the aid of quilts and blankets, transforms our nursery into a stage. I am also the one who decides how the performers' make-up, hair and costumes will be done. I am the only one with any experience of all this.

By the evening everything is ready, even so, and the play can begin. The audience consists of Father, Mother, Aunt, the governess, the housekeeper and a couple of the maids. They all sit together in a narrow doorway and I doubt they can see much of what happens on stage, but it does not seem to matter. They clearly have a very good time, regardless.

We have a young girl of twelve lodging with us. She is very sweet and wears my mother's old ballgown to play the part of the lady love, 'my rose in the forest'. My elder sister, who is also twelve, is dressed in my father's oldest uniform jacket and plays the suitor. She is very pretty, too, and she acts so well. She has a real talent for acting. Our nursemaid plays an old housekeeper and as for me, I play an old man of seventy. There is meant to be an old man with long white hair in the play and I take that role because my hair is long and very white.

We are a big, big hit! I wonder what the author would have said, if he had seen his play performed in that way. But perhaps he too would have been content.

From that day onwards, I no longer dream only of writing novels. Now I want to write plays as well. I long to be older, so that I am no longer obliged to sit at my school desk and waste my time on arithmetic and translations.

*

It is a fine spring afternoon and I am walking to and fro in the spinney behind the garden. As soon as one of the meandering paths leads me to the spinney's edge, I emerge into an abundance of light. Big fields spread out before me and the sunlight is held there, cradled in the moisture rising from the freshly ploughed ground. In one spot the air is gleaming like purple, in another it appears to be full of gold dust. Back in amongst the trees, it is surprisingly dark. Their leaves have only recently unfurled. I have not had time to get used to the green darkness that prevails beneath them. Suddenly, as I turn into the shadow from the light at the boundary of the garden, I find two rhyming lines on my tongue.

It is so dark beneath the linden trees
So anxiously quieten'd in the still breeze

What now? What is this? I stand transfixed, the surprise taking my breath away. This is surely verse? Can I write in verse?

I am fifteen years old and I have read all the books of poetry in our home. Tegnér, Runeberg, Mrs Lenngren, Stagnelius, Vitalis, Bellman, Wallin, Dahlgren, but it has never occurred to me that I would be able to write poetry myself. Writing poetry, that was something elevated and sacred. It was a gift only bestowed on select members of humanity.

But now at least I have composed a rhyming couplet. I repeat the lines over and over. I say them out loud to myself. I give them a musical lilt. But I do not attempt to add any more. I am far too astonished by what has happened to me.

Imagine that you have grown up as a poor beggar child and suddenly someone comes and announces you are of royal birth!

Imagine that you were blind and suddenly started to see, that you were miserably poor and came into riches at a stroke, that you were a friendless outcast and stumbled into deep, warm love! Imagine what you will by way of great and unanticipated happiness, and you will still not conceive of anything as vast as what I felt at that moment.

I can rhyme; I can write in verse. I have the same gift as Tegnér, Runeberg, Wallin. I shall become like one of them.

I have always intended to write novels and plays. But this is not as remarkable as writing in verse. It is merely pleasurable and entertaining, but verse, that is the pinnacle. It is the route to glory. It is the most wondrous thing of all.

I conceal my great discovery from my whole family. But I feel giddy all evening, not attending to the remarks addressed to me and giving back-to-front answers.

I still remember us that day, sitting round the table for our evening meal. There sits Father, and there sits Mother. There are my sisters, my aunt, the governess. And there am I, small and pale with lots of white-blonde hair, just like any other girl. Father takes the lead as usual, joking with Aunt and the governess. The mood is cheerful and happy and the conversation dwells on the most everyday things. What would they have said, the others, if they had had an inkling of the irrepressible hopes running wild inside my head?

My one slight concern is Aunt Wennervik's prophecy. There was nothing in it about my becoming great or remarkable. But anyone who writes poetry is a great figure. They are all but superior to a king. I start to fear that I have been mistaken and do not have the divine gift after all.

Then I repeat to myself the little rhyming verse and once more feel immensely proud, immensely happy.

When night finally comes, I want to test what my new ability amounts to, and I embark hopefully on writing a poem. I bind and connect word to word and do not sleep a wink all night. I join line of verse to line of verse and have a whole host of stanzas ready before morning.

But the poem is not the remarkable part for me. The remarkable part is that I have the ability, that I can write in rhyme and that I belong among the chosen.

After that I compose verse at all times of day, early and late, day and night, for many years.

Most of this poetic production has been destroyed and the small amount that remains is very feeble. Of all this authorship there is only one little bit that I am happy with, and occasionally whisper to myself as I stand beneath the dark canopy of the trees and see the light of the evening sun as it sets plains and valleys ablaze.

> It is so dark beneath the linden trees
> So anxiously quieten'd in the still breeze

*

I am twenty-three years old, and I am in Stockholm, back at the good home that took me in when I was a child of nine. I am staying there while I make my application to the women's teacher training college. I have sat my examinations and the following day finds me waiting to hear whether I have passed and will be offered a place at the college.

It is a long day and almost impossible to bring to a close. We had examinations for the best part of a week and it was not as hard as I had feared it would be. These were days filled with extreme tension but things happened, there was contest and competition and at times even some fun. All the examiners were full of goodwill and their demands were not excessive. Overall, I think I acquitted myself well in the tests. But unfortunately acquitting yourself well is not enough. You must also be better than a lot of other people.

Only twenty-five students are admitted to the college each year, and there are forty-nine applicants. That is the terrifying part. We were questioned in small groups of three, so I do not know how the others fared in the test. But I am sure that all the others went to proper schools in towns. They have not lived their entire lives out in the country and spent all their spare time writing useless poetry. It is only natural for every single one of them to be more knowledgeable than me.

I have spent this past year in Stockholm, taking a course to prepare myself for the entrance examinations. But that is just one year I have devoted to serious study. The others have completed eight years at leading grammar schools.

I have been informed that we will not be told the outcome until late in the afternoon. If I have been unsuccessful then at that point a messenger will come with a letter, telling me that I cannot be taken on as a student at the teacher training college this year. If I have been successful, on the other hand, I will not receive the letter, or indeed any other form of communication. Then I can safely make my way to the college the next morning and commence my studies. But it is still only the middle of the day. There are many hours to go before I can start expecting the messenger with the dreaded letter.

My relations feel decidedly sorry for me, but what can they do to help? We sit around talking, but I find it hard to follow what they say. My mind keeps going back to speculating whether I solved that mathematics problem entirely incorrectly or gave the wrong answer to one of the Swedish questions.

And I hope and pray that I will pass the examinations, not

because I am more learned than my fellow applicants, but because I need to pass more than anyone else.

This is one thing of which I am certain, you see. No one else has a greater need than I do of being admitted as a student to benefit from the three years of free tuition offered by the training college. If I fail to get in, it will be the end of me. I will have to try for some little position as a governess with a salary of a few hundred kronor, or I will have to go back home and help in the household. I am no longer as childish as when I lived at home before and believed wishing and dreaming were enough to make you into someone. Now I know that I must work and acquire knowledge if I want to be a writer.

I also know that I will need knowledge if I want to live. We have been so poor at home these past few years. I must learn to earn my own keep, if I do not want to sink into misfortune.

Perhaps the other applicants are not acting entirely against their fathers' wishes. Perhaps they have not had to insist so forcefully on being allowed to leave home. Perhaps in their homes the belief does not persist that a woman has no need to learn anything properly. And if they do not get a place now, perhaps they will be able to make another attempt next year. But I will never again get Father's permission to come to Stockholm and study, if I fail this time.

The others are probably not as poor as I am, either. Perhaps they can get some assistance to study at other schools. But I cannot. Father has no money to give me, and that probably goes a long way to explain his opposition to my leaving home. But if only I can get into the training college, I will have a secure future ahead of me and then I will certainly be able to borrow money so I can support myself in Stockholm for the duration of the course. But if I fail, who will want to help me then?

How slowly time is passing today. And I have no way of keeping myself busy. I cannot go out for a walk, for just imagine if the messenger were to bring the letter while I was out! And reading or studying is pointless. The examination is over, after all. There is nothing to do but wait.

I have spent my whole life waiting, only in a different way. I have been waiting to be discovered, waiting for someone to come and read my novels, my poems, my plays, and find them beautiful and brilliant. Every time I showed them to anybody, I held out the hope that this miracle would happen.

And on one occasion, it very nearly did. There was a wedding at one of the neighbours' and I was a bridesmaid. At the wedding dinner, one of the groom's male attendants read out a tribute in verse to the bridesmaids, and I gave the thank-you speech to the attendants, also in verse. Both of us won high praise for this, of course. Verse written for special occasions is always very well received.

Shortly after the meal, Mother came over to say that Eva Frxyell* wanted to speak to me.

Eva Fryxell was the daughter of the great historian Anders Fryxell, who was the dean of the parish adjoining ours. She herself was a writer and moreover a highly educated lady. She was in the habit of spending her winters in Stockholm, where she moved in the literary circles of the time. No one could be more appropriate than she in helping me on my way in the world.

She was one of the wedding guests. She had heard me read my verses aloud and now she wished to speak to me.

She enquired whether I often wrote poetry. She asked me to send her my best pieces, so that she could try to get them published in some magazine.

She was very encouraging and I thought that my luck had finally turned. I sent her my poems and began the wait to see them in print.

But the whole autumn went by, the whole winter, and there was no word of them.

It was spring by the time a letter came from Eva Fryxell, and it was a thick one. She had sent back my poems. No magazine had been willing to accept them. But she had more to say than that. She wrote that I should get out into the world and gain some knowledge, otherwise I would never make anything of myself.

And it was perhaps not least her urging that had made me decide, last year, to break away from home. I had done no writing of my own all year but concentrated on my studies to acquire all the knowledge that I lacked.

It was a process that aroused a love of studying in me. I yearned for those three years at the training college, for those three years of hard, intensive work and progress.

'She will toil and labour all her days,' Aunt Wennervik had said, and I very much hoped that this would be the case.

The doorbell in the hall rings occasionally. Every time it makes me jump and wonder if it is the messenger from the training college. I have been assured that he won't come until after five o'clock, but who can say? Perhaps this year they reached their final decision earlier.

My hopes are dwindling with every moment that passes. Of course the other forty-eight have done better than I have. And of course I gave the wrong answer multiple times, without even noticing.

The clock strikes three. There is another ring at the door.

It is a relative of mine, a fellow student. She has also applied to the college this year, and we were both in the same group answering examination questions.

She has come up to tell me that we have both been given places. She is unwilling to say how she found out, but the information has come from a reliable source. And as soon as she heard, she hurried here to bring me word, so I would not have to sit worrying any longer.

I do not know what I am saying or doing. I have no idea if I thank her. I slip away to the very back of the apartment, to be on my own.

I cannot control myself. I shake and tremble and cannot keep still. And I am in floods of tears.

I sense that I have surmounted the greatest obstacle of all. I am no longer helpless and dependent. I have a career ahead of me. I shall be able to earn my own living and be in control of my own actions. It will be my own responsibility to go as far as I wish to.

*

I am at the Grand Hotel in Jerusalem, one evening in March

1900. I have been called out of my room by Jemil, our Syrian dragoman, to receive a guest. This guest cannot be shown into my room, nor into the big guest lounge. The dragoman does not feel able to bring him any further than the entrance hall of the hotel.

It really is no wonder, either, for the visitor does not look entirely appealing. He is an old black man of a less than attractive type, a man with very full lips and long arms, his swelling muscles, heavy body and coarse, bark-like skin giving the impression that he belongs to the human race that existed before the Flood. And this figure is not covered in anything that could be referred to as clothes. He is swathed and wrapped in long, grubby white strips of cloth, and over his head he has thrown a trailing end of the same cloth.*

A few days before this, Jemil was taking me and my fellow traveller Sophie Elkan* through the old mosque of El Aksa in Jerusalem, and in a side aisle we were surprised to come across some ragged bedding spread in a window niche. Jemil said that this niche was generally occupied by a soothsayer, who offered his services in predicting the future to the passing public. I was sorry not to find him in residence just then. I would have liked to have my fortune told by a proper soothsayer in the old El Aksa, which was built on the foundations of Solomon's temple. Now our kindly dragoman had gone to find the soothsayer and brought him to the hotel, so I could have my fortune told in Jerusalem after all.

It is not as impressive to have my fortune told in the entrance hall of the hotel, with a stream of servants and travellers coming and going, as in the El-Aksa Mosque, but I have no choice. The three of us go over to a table in a nook. The soothsayer takes out a bag that he has kept concealed under his strips of cloth, unties it and pours a considerable layer of sand onto the table, unmistakeably some kind of sand from the sea, as it is full of little bits of broken seashell.

As he makes these preparations, I cannot help thinking of Aunt Wennervik. I wonder whether this Eastern gentleman will prove as good a seer as she was.

Once the dark-skinned soothsayer has spread his sand

evenly, he says some words in Arabic, which the dragoman translates into English.

'Madame, he asks you to think of some topic on which you seek enlightenment. You are not to say what it is, only to hold it in your mind for a time, and then you will get an answer.'

For a few moments, I am nonplussed. Is there not an unbridgeable gulf between an Arab soothsayer and a Western traveller? We have lived in entirely separate worlds. What can I ask about that will not be beyond the sphere in which his thoughts normally move?

I have spent my whole stay in Jerusalem thinking of essentially one thing. I have come here solely to visit some farmers from Näs in Dalarna province, who have moved here and set up a colony with a band of Americans. I wanted to see them so I could write a book about them.

I have now been to see them many times, eaten at their table, visited their schools, watched them at their labour in their workshops, taken rides in their home-constructed carts and carriages, walked on carpets and sat on chairs that they have made themselves. I have heard them speak of their faith openly and directly. I have found nothing about them that is not good, sincere and heartfelt.

I felt deeply moved to see their benign Swedish faces and hear their honest Swedish tongue in this foreign land. I have experienced their church services and heard them sing a song of farewell, 'We shall meet again,' to us, their Swedish guests. We have found them unpretentious, hardworking, patient, and I am burning with desire to write about them.

But at the same time I have started to wonder whether I shall ever be able to write a book about them. It is not only fear of my own inability to deal with the subject that makes me dubious; there are other reasons, too. I live every day in a state of doubt and indecision that is almost painful.

It is rooted in something that is a very serious matter to me. This long journey will have been in vain if I cannot write the book. Time, effort, money, thrown away to no effect. This is nothing that can be dismissed lightly.

I ask myself every day: Will this turn into a book? Will it

ever be written? Will anyone want to read it?

But can I ask a black soothsayer about this? Has such a human being from an ancestral time ever seen a book? Does he know what a novel is?

In any case, there is nothing else I wish to know just now, and I fix my thoughts on this: 'Will I succeed in writing a book about the Swedish farmers in Jerusalem?'

The soothsayer raises his hand over the sand that he has spread in front of him, reaches out a large index finger with a long, curved fingernail and makes several rows of holes in the sand. He mutters and counts. Quite a long time passes before he says anything. But then he turns to Jemil and says something in Arabic.

'He says Madame is thinking of something that she intends to write on a sheet of paper,' translates Jemil. 'He asks the lady not to be uneasy. She will succeed in the project she has in mind.'*

I cannot help but be a little astonished by his answer. He seems to know how to read minds, this outlandish man.

He eyes me expectantly and I ask the dragoman to tell him that he has given me a proper answer and I am very pleased with him.

The soothsayer immediately smooths out the little holes in the sand so it is nice and even all over and then invites me to ask another question.

This time I need no lengthy meditations. We are to leave Jerusalem the next day and travel on to Nazareth, Tiberias, Damascus. All I ask is: 'Will our journey go well? Will we get to the places we want to see?'

This time it does not take the soothsayer long to speak, either. He does not answer my question, however, but asks to see my hands, both my hands.

I hold out my hands, palms uppermost. The soothsayer studies them, takes one step back and raises his arms. The words come pouring from his lips. He is plainly excited.

'What has got into him? What is he saying?' I ask the dragoman.

'He says that Madame is thinking of a road that lies ahead

of her,' he replies, 'and he says that Madame will have a good journey. He says that Madame has the signs of Sultan Ibrahim il Kalil and of Sultan Soliman on her hands. He says that Madame will succeed at everything. You are under a very strong star, Madame.'

I ask the dragoman to tell the soothsayer that I am very content with his answers, and I give him his payment. I realise that, having now learned I have the signs of Abraham and Solomon in my hands, I truly ought to be content.

'I wonder what Aunt Wennervik would say about that?' I ask myself as I go back to my room.

No sooner have I said the words than I think I hear a brisk, no-nonsense voice speaking right into my ear in a homely Värmland accent: 'I'm sure you know, my girl, that despite the way they look and the rags they wear, these Easterners know more about flattery and compliments than the rest of us, especially if there's money in it. But you can trust my prophecy. That one wasn't paid for. You will travel, you will work, you will write books, you will never be in entirely good health, and that is the way your life will run.'

'Dear Aunt Wennervik,' I whisper back, 'Don't worry! You haven't understood what this man means by his words. He is simply saying that anyone who finds themselves able in mature years to carry through what they dreamed of as a child has been granted the luck of the wise ancients and has been under the guidance of a good star.'

(From *Troll och människor*, 1915.)

Notes

32 *Två spådomar*: the original Swedish version opens with a note: 'Commissioned by my German publisher in November 1908.' The story covers some of the ground that Lagerlöf went on to develop in her autobiographical Mårbacka trilogy, particularly the middle volume, *Ett barns memorarer*, written in 1930. This was most recently translated as *Memoirs of a Child*, Norvik Press, 2022.

36 *Oceola*: sometimes spelled *Osceola*, this was an undistinguished but popular adventure novel by William Mayne Reid, published in 1858, its protagonist a heroic Native American.

36 *Nösselt's General History for Women*: this was a multi-part work, translated from the German and published in Swedish in 1861-2.

36 The texts listed are:

Fritiof's Saga: a cycle of poems derived from an Old Norse saga about a Viking hero, written by Esias Tegnér between 1820 and 1825;

Andersen's Fairy Tales: Danish writer Hans Christian Andersen began publishing volumes of his subsequently world-renowned *Eventyr* in 1835;

The Tales of Ensign Stål: *Fänrik Ståls sägner* (1848-60) is a cycle of Romantic nationalist poems celebrating bravery of soldiers in war, by the Finland-Swedish author Johan Ludvig Runeberg.

38 *close relations*: the young Selma stayed with her uncle and aunt, Oriel and Georgina Afzelius, and their children Elin and Allan.

39 The plays listed are:

The African Woman: *L'Africaine*, a French grand opera from 1865 with music by Giacomo Meyerbeer and a libretto by Eugène Scribe;

Robert: *Robert Le Diable*, opera by Giacomo Meyerbeer, premiered in 1831, in Paris;

The Mute Girl: *La muette de Portici*, also sometimes called *Masaniello*, a French grand opera by Daniel Auber premiered in 1828, in Paris;

The Marksman: *Der Freischütz*, German Romantic opera by Carl Maria von Weber with a libretto by Friedrich Kind, premiered in 1821 in Berlin;

The Värmlanders: *Värmlänningarna,* a piece of musical theatre and burlesque comedy written in 1846 by Fredrik August Dahlgren with musical assistance from Andreas Randel;

Fair Helen: *La belle Helène*, an operetta by Jacques Offenbach with libretto by Henri Meilhac and Ludovic Halévy, premiered in 1864 in Paris;

The School for Wives: *L'École des Femmes*, theatrical comedy by the seventeenth-century French playwright Molière;

Hotbed Flowers: *Blommor i drivbänk* by Sweden's Frans Hedberg was a popular comedy critical of education in girls' boarding schools, premiered at the Royal Opera in Stockholm in 1862;

My Rose in the Forest: *Min ros i skogen*, was a comedy originally written in German by Wolfgang Müller von Königswinter under the title *Sie hat ihr Herz entdeckt*. It was adapted into Swedish and widely performed in Sweden from 1867 onwards.

46 *Eva Fryxell*: Eva Fryxell (1829-1920) was a literary critic, author and artist, and an active member of the women's movement. Her father, Professor Anders Fryxell (1795-1881), was a historian, educator and clergyman. He and his daughter were good friends and mentors to Selma from her childhood onwards.

48 *This guest cannot be shown into my room ... a trailing end of the same cloth*. Although this description, and some of the subsequent references to this individual, will offend twenty-first century sensibilities, Lagerlöf is here reflecting widespread European assumptions and biases of the period in which she was writing.

48 *Sophie Elkan*: Elkan (1853-1921) was a fellow author and a close friend of Selma Lagerlöf, her confidante and companion over many years. Their relationship is charted in their correspondence, published in Ying Töijer-Nilsson's *Du lär mig att bli fri* (Albert Bonniers förlag,1992, You Teach Me to Be Free).

50 *She will succeed in the project she has in mind*. Lagerlöf did write and publish her novel about the pious Swedish farmers who left their lives in Dalarna to go and settle in the Holy Land under the title *Jerusalem*, in two volumes (1901 and 1902).

MISS FREDRIKA

Mamsell Fredrika

Translated by Sarah Death

It was one Christmas night, a proper Yule night.

The trolls raised the rock platforms on tall gold pillars and held their midwinter festival. The Christmas elf danced around the rice pudding in his new red cap. Old gods circled the fortress in grey storm capes, and the Hell Horse* stood in Österhaninge* churchyard. He scraped the frozen ground with his hooves. He was marking out the place for a new grave.

Not far from there, at old Årsta manor house, Miss Fredrika* lay sleeping. As everyone knows, Årsta manor house has long been haunted, but Miss Fredrika's sleep was sound and peaceful. She had grown old now and was worn out after many arduous working days and many long journeys – she had virtually circumnavigated the world, after all – and she had returned to her childhood home to find repose.

Outside the manor, a lively fanfare rang out. Death had mounted his grey steed and come riding up to the front gate. His wide scarlet coat and the proud plume in his hat streamed out in the night-time wind. The stern knight wished to conquer a romantic heart and that was why he made his appearance in such rarely seen finery.

Wasted effort, lord knight, wasted effort! The front gate is shut and the lady your heart desires is deep in slumber. You must find a better opportunity and a more suitable time. Look out for her when she sets off for the early service, stern lord knight, look out for her on the road to church!

*

Old Miss Fredrika slept soundly in her beloved home. No one better deserved the sweetness of rest than she. Like a Christmas angel she had recently sat in a circle of children and told them the story of Jesus and the shepherds, the telling of her story making her eyes gleam and completely transfiguring her wizened face. Now that she had attained old age, no one made derogatory comments about Fredrika's appearance. On the contrary, those who encountered the slight and diminutive figure, her delicate little hands and wise, kindly face were eager to retain the image in their minds as the most delightful recollection.

In Miss Fredrika's large room among many relics and mementos there was a dried-up little bush. It was the Rose of Jericho that Miss Fredrika had brought back with her from the distant lands of the East. Now, on this Christmas night, it came into bloom, entirely of its own accord. The dry sticks were covered in red buds that shimmered like fiery sparks, illuminating the whole room.

The light of the sparks glimmered on a small, frail lady, advanced in years, seated in the big yellow armchair to give an audience. It could not be Miss Fredrika herself, for she was sound asleep, and yet it was. She was holding a reception for her memories; the room was full of them. People and homes and objects and thoughts and debates converged through the air. Memories of her childhood and of her youth, love and tears, honours and bitter scorn, all swooped in on the pale figure, who surveyed the whole scene from her seat with a benign smile. She had words of jest or melancholy for them all.

At night, all things assume their rightful character and form. And just as it is only then that we can see the stars in the heavens, on Earth too we see much that is never visible to us by day. So now, in the glow of the red buds on the Rose of Jericho, many singular figures could be seen in Miss Fredrika's salon. Among them were the rigid 'ma chère mère', the good-natured Beata Hvardagslag, people from both Orient and Occident, dreamy Nina, and energetic, forceful Hertha, dressed all in white.*

'Can anyone tell me why that woman always has to be in white?' joked the diminutive figure in the armchair, catching sight of her.

But all the memories spoke to the old lady, saying, 'Look upon all that you have seen and experienced, all that you have achieved, all the causes you have served. Are you not tired, do you not wish to rest?'

'Not yet,' replied the shadow in the yellow armchair. 'I have one book left to write.* I cannot take my rest before it is finished.'

With that, the shadows vanished. The Rose of Jericho shrivelled, and the yellow armchair stood empty.

*

In Österhaninge church, the dead were celebrating midnight mass. One of them stepped up to the bells and rang in Christmas, another went round lighting the Christmas candles, and a third began playing the organ with bony fingers. Through the wide-open doors, the rest of those emerging from the night and the graves crowded into the bright and radiant House of the Lord. They appeared as they had been in life, merely a shade paler. They opened the doors of the pews with jangling keys and whispered and tattled as they came up the aisle.

'These are all the candles, now burning in God's house, that *she* gave to the poor.'

'We lie warm in our graves for as long as *she* gives clothes and firewood to the poor.'

'Look at that, she has spoken so many words powerful enough to open human hearts and now those words are our pew keys.'

'She has thought beautiful thoughts about God's love. Those thoughts have raised us from our graves.'

This was what they tattled and whispered before they took their seats in the pews and bowed their pale brows in their wrinkled hands in prayer.

*

Meanwhile at Årsta, someone entered Miss Fredrika's room and put a kindly hand on the sleeping lady's arm.

'Up with you, my Fredrika! It is time to set off for the early service.'

Old Miss Fredrika opened her eyes and saw her beloved sister Agathe, the one who had died, standing by the bed with a candle in her hand. She had no trouble recognising her, for she looked just as she had done here on Earth. Miss Fredrika did not take fright but was only too glad to see the loved one by whose side she wanted to spend the long slumber.

She got out of bed and dressed hurriedly. There was no time for conversation; the carriage was at the front gate. The others must have gone on ahead, for only Miss Fredrika and her dead sister were moving about the house.

'Do you remember, Fredrika,' said her sister, once they were in their seats and the carriage was rattling briskly along the road to the service, 'do you remember the way you would always sit here waiting for some knight to abduct you on the way to church?'

'I am still waiting,' said old Miss Fredrika and laughed. 'I never make this journey without keeping a lookout for my knight.'

But hurry as they might, they still arrived too late. The vicar was descending from the pulpit as they came into the church, and the closing hymn began. Never had Miss Fredrika heard such glorious singing. It was as if both Earth and Heaven were lending their voices, as if every pew and stone and length of wood were joining in.

She had never seen the church so crammed full: there were people sitting on the altar rail and the steps of the pulpit; they were squeezed together in the pews, and the road outside was packed with those who could not get in. Yet the sisters found a place, even so; the crowd made way for them.

'Fredrika,' said her sister, 'look at the people!'

And Miss Fredrika looked and looked.

Then she realised that she, like the woman in the folk tale, had happened on the mass of the dead.* A cold shiver ran down her spine but, as often before, she felt more curious than frightened.

And now she saw the individuals who made up the crowd in the church. They were all women: stooped, grey figures with rounded collars and washed-out mantillas, with hats that had lost their sheen and dresses that had been turned or looked distinctly shabby. She saw a vast number of lined faces, shrunken mouths, fogged spectacles and wrinkled hands, yet not a single hand bearing two plain rings.

And yes, now Miss Fredrika understood. These were all the now-departed spinsters in the land of Sweden, holding midnight mass in Österhaninge church.

Then her dead sister leaned towards her.

'Sister, do you regret what you did for all of these, your sisters?'

'No', said Miss Fredrika. 'What have I to gladden my heart besides having been granted the privilege of working for them? I once sacrificed my reputation as an author for them.* It gratifies me that I knew what I was sacrificing but did it, even so.'

'Then you can stay and hear more,' said her sister.

At that moment someone spoke from over in the choir, in a voice that was gentle but clear.

'My sisters,' said the voice, 'our pitiable breed, derided and ill-educated, will soon exist no more. God has wished us to die out from this Earth.'

'Dear friends, we shall soon be nothing but a fable. The number of unwanted spinsters has reached its limit. Death is on horseback, patrolling the road to the church to meet the last of us. Before the next midnight mass she will be dead, the last of the old maids.

'Sisters, sisters! We were the solitary ones here on Earth. Slighted at parties and serving thanklessly in countless homes. Scorn and lovelessness hung about us. Our way through life was hard, and our name was synonymous with ridicule.

'But God has shown mercy.

'To *one* of us He gave strength and genius. To one of us He gave an endless supply of goodness. To one of us He gave the glorious gift of words. She became all that we should have been. She illuminated our dismal fates. She took the role of maidservant in the home, as we had done, but she gave her gifts to thousands of homes. She nursed the sick, as we had done, but she fought the terrible plague of prejudice. She told her stories to thousands of children. She had friends among the needy in every land. She gave her gifts from fuller hands than we could and with a warmer disposition. There was no room in her heart for any of our bitterness, for she loved it away. Her honour has been like that of a queen. She has borne aloft the treasure of gratitude from a million hearts. Her words have carried weight in the great questions of humanity. Her name has sounded through the New World and the Old. And yet she is naught but an old maid.'

'She has shone a light on our dark fates. Blessings be upon her name!'

And the dead chimed in, echoing a thousandfold: 'Blessings be upon her name!'

'Sister,' whispered Miss Fredrika, 'can you not forbid them from making me the conceited, poor, sinful mortal that I am?'

'But sisters, sisters,' said the voice in conclusion, 'she has turned upon our breed with all the power she possesses. At her calls for freedom and work for all, the scorned old paupers living on charity have died out. She has broken down the barriers of tyranny around children. She has sent out young girls into fully active lives. She has brought an end to the solitude, ignorance and joylessness. Miserable and despised old maids with no purpose or content to their lives will no longer exist, no more of the likes of us.'

Again the echo of the shadowy figures rang out, as exultant as a hunting song in the forest, as the shouts of a happy crowd of children: 'Blessed be her memory!'

With that, the dead swarmed out of the church and Miss Fredrika wiped a tear from the corner of her eye.

'I shall not be coming home with you,' said her dead sister. 'Don't you feel an urge to stay out here, too?'

'Oh yes, I do, but I cannot. There is a book I must finish first.'

'Well then, good night, and watch out for the knight on

the road from the church,' said her dead sister, giving that mischievous smile, just as she used to.

Then Miss Fredrika was taken home. The whole of Årsta still slept and she went quietly up to her room, lay down and fell asleep at once.

*

A few hours later, she was taken to the real early service. She travelled in a closed carriage, but she let down the window to look at the stars; it was also possible that she was spying out for her knight, the way she had done in the old days.

And there he was, galloping up to the carriage window. How splendidly he was seated on his prancing steed. His scarlet coat flapped in the wind. His pale countenance was stern but beautiful.

'Will you be mine?' he whispered.

Her old heart was entranced by the tall figure with the fluttering hat plume. She forgot that she needed to live for another year.

'I am ready,' she whispered.

'Then I will come and collect you a week from now, in your father's house.'

He bent down and kissed her and with that, he vanished; but the kiss of death left her shivering with cold.

A short while later, Miss Fredrika was seated in the church, in the same place she had occupied as a child. Here she forgot both the knight and the spirits and sat smiling in quiet rapture at the thought of the revelation of God's glory.

But either she was tired because she had not slept all night, or the warmth and close atmosphere and smoking candles had a soporific effect on her, as on many others. She dozed off, just for a second, she simply could not help it.

And perhaps it was the case that God wished to open the portal to the land of dreams to her.

In that single second of slumber, she saw her exacting father, her beautiful, elegant mother and plain little Petrea* sitting there in the church. And the child's soul was crushed by an anguish greater than that experienced by any fully-grown person. The vicar stood in the pulpit and spoke of a stern, punitive God, and the child was pale and shaking, as if the words were axe blows, cleaving her heart.

'Oh, what a God, what a terrible God!'

The next second she was awake, but still she shivered and shuddered as she had after death's kiss on the road from church. Her heart was once again trapped in the wild sorrow of her childhood.

Suddenly she was in such haste that she felt an urge to rush out of the church. She had to get home and write her book, her magnificent book about the God of peace and love.

*

Nothing else that would now seem worthy of note happened to Miss Fredrika before New Year's Eve. Life and death, just as day and night, prevailed in quiet concord over the Earth in that last week of the year, but when New Year's Eve came, death took up the staff of authority and declared that Miss Fredrika would now belong to him.

If only this had been generally known, then assuredly the entire population of Sweden would have sent up a collective prayer to God, asking to keep among them their purest soul, their warmest heart. Then people would have kept vigils of anxious concern in many homes in many countries, where she had left loving hearts. Then the poor, the sick and the afflicted would have forgotten their own plight to remember hers, and then all the children, now grown up in the blessing of her deeds, would have clasped their hands to pray for another year for their best friend. A year, so she would be able to insert the keystone in her life's work and reveal it in its full clarity.

For death was drawing close to Miss Fredrika.

There was a storm raging outside that New Year's night, and a storm raging inside Miss Fredrika, too. She felt all the torments of life and death clashing inside her.

'What agony!' she sighed. 'What agony!'

But the agony abated, and peace came, and she whispered

gently: 'The love of Christ – the best love – the peace of God – eternal light!'

And yes, that was what she would have wished to write in her book, and perhaps many other glorious and lovely things. Who knows? We know only one thing for certain: that books fade from memory, but a life such as hers is never forgotten.

The old seeress's eyes closed and she lost herself in visions.

Her body did battle with death, but she was not aware of it. Her closest relations sat around her deathbed and wept, but she did not see them. Her spirit had already embarked on its ascent.

Now dreams became reality for her and reality a dream. Now the version of herself she had already seen in the vision of her youth stood waiting at Heaven's gate with a countless host of the dead around her. And Heaven was opened to them. He, the One, the bringer of salvation, stood at its open gate. And His infinite love aroused in the waiting spirits and in her a longing to fly into His embrace, and their longing carried them and her, and they were borne as if on wings upwards, upwards.

The next day there was sorrow in the land of Sweden, sorrow in many parts of the world.

Fredrika Bremer was dead.

(From *Osynliga länkar*, 1894.)

Notes

54 *Hell Horse*: in Swedish folklore, this 'Hell Horse' (Helhästen) was a supernatural figure in the shape of a three-legged horse, foretelling the death of anyone who happened to meet him.

54 *Österhaninge*: part of the Haninge municipality to the south of Stockholm and the parish in which Fredrika Bremer's childhood home Årsta slott (Årsta manor house) stands to this day.

54 *Miss Fredrika*: Fredrika Bremer (1801-65), was a bestselling novelist, intrepid traveller, and campaigner for social justice and women's suffrage. She also fought for

international copyright laws to prevent pirated publications and unauthorised translations.

56 *Among them were the rigid 'ma chère mère' […] and energetic, forceful Hertha in her white attire*: these are all protagonists of Bremer's novels.

56 *I have one book left to write*: this refers to a long-planned autobiographical novel, provisionally entitled *Aurora*, unfinished fragments of which were in existence at Bremer's death. Along with many other papers that passed into the hands of her sister Charlotte Quiding, the manuscript was in all probability burned by Charlotte and her husband Peter. See Carina Burman: *Bremer. En biografi*. Albert Bonniers förlag, 2001, p. 494.

58 *like the woman in the folk tale, had happened on the mass of the dead*: there are many recorded instances of the tale of the Christmas mass of the dead in Nordic folklore. The online Map of Nordic Legends (Sägenkartan) produced by the Institute for Language and Folklore in Sweden (ISOF) and its Norwegian and Finnish counterparts shows numerous examples from regions including Halland, Dalarna and multiple localities in Lagerlöf's Värmland. Two of the versions feature in English translation in Anna Maria Hellberg Moberg's volume *Swedish Folk Tales* (History Press, 2024).

58 *I once sacrificed my reputation as an author for them*: this could refer to the reception of Bremer's novel *Hertha*. The eponymous heroine of her 1856 novel is uncompromising in her fight for women's rights and alienated some readers who were more accustomed to the less demanding family novels of her earlier writing career.

60 *plain little Petrea*: Petrea is a character in Bremer's novel *Hemmet, eller, familje-sorger och fröjder* (1839, translated by Mary Howitt as *The Home, or, Family Cares and Family Joys,* 1843) about a family with numerous children growing to adulthood. The account of Petrea's struggles to become a published writer is unmistakeably autobiographical.

Landscapes, Families and 'Others'

GOD'S PEACE AT CHRISTMAS

Gudsfreden

Translated by Linda Schenck

Once upon a time on a Christmas Eve, with the kind of heavy sky that foreboded a huge snowstorm, and a piercing northerly wind, there was an old farmstead. It was that pivotal time of the afternoon when everyone was hurrying to finish their labors so that they could go to the bathhouse and make themselves clean for the holidays. The bathhouse fire was roaring and so intense that a flame shot up through the chimney and an endless array of sparks and flakes of soot flew through the air, landing on the snow-covered roofs of the outbuildings.

The flame rising from the chimney of the bathhouse and hovering like a pillar of fire over the farm made everyone keenly aware that Christmas was at hand. The housemaid scrubbing the floor of the entrance hall found herself singing under her breath in spite of the layer of ice forming across the top of her scrub bucket. The farmhands chopping Christmas firewood in the woodshed started splitting two logs at a time and swinging their axes with such gusto their exertions seemed like child's play.

An old woman emerged from the baking shed with a big pile of round Christmas loaves in her arms. She crossed the yard cautiously and entered the red farmhouse, walking into the main room and setting the bread down on the buffet with care. Then she opened a folded tablecloth, spread it over the table and set the loaves, a larger and a smaller one together, at intervals along the table. She was a peculiar, homely old woman with reddish hair, heavy eyelids and an unusual, austere set to her mouth and chin, as if the tendons in her throat were foreshortened. But now, on Christmas Eve, there was such a sense of serenity and gaiety about her it was impossible to think of her as the least bit unattractive.

And yet there was one person on the farm who was anything but happy. This was the young housemaid whose task it was to prepare the birch switch bundles for use in the bathhouse. She was sitting by the hearth with a fine load of birch branches at her feet, but no decent twigs with which to tie the bundles. The main room had a long, low window with small panes through which the gleam from the bathhouse shone into the room, casting shadows on the floor and gilding the branches.

The housemaid's unhappiness increased in proportion to the height of the flames, because she knew the switches were sure to fall apart the moment they were raised, and that she would be put to shame for her work, at least until next year's Christmas log fire was burning in that chimney.

Just as she sat there feeling miserable, the person by whom she was most intimidated entered the room. This was Ingmar Ingmarsson himself, master of the house. He was undoubtedly on his way in from checking that the fire in the bathhouse would be sufficiently hot, and now he was wanting to see how the birch switches were coming along. He was an old man, Ingmar Ingmarsson, and he liked things to be done in the traditional way. Because people were, in fact, starting to set aside the old ways of having a Christmas bath in the bathhouse and slapping each other with birch switches, it had become very important to him that this ritual be maintained on his farm, and be carried out properly.

Ingmar Ingmarsson was wearing an old sheepskin coat, leather trousers and untanned brogues. He was untidy and unshaven, his demeanor leisurely. He entered the room so discreetly one might have taken him for a mendicant. His features and general appearance were more or less as unappealing as those of his wife, to whom he was related by blood. The housemaid had learned from an early age to show the utmost respect for everyone who bore these traits. It was considered a sign of greatness simply to be descended from the ancient Ingmarsson lineage, the family that had always been the most high-born in the community. And indeed, the greatest person was Ingmar Ingmarsson himself, the wealthiest, wisest and mightiest man in the entire parish.

Ingmar Ingmarsson approached the maid, bent down and raised up one of her switches, drawing it through the air. Instantly, the branches flew apart. One landed on the banquet table, another in the canopied bed.

'Good grief, young lady,' chuckled Ingmar Ingmarsson, 'can you imagine that switches like these could ever be used in the Ingmarssons' bathhouse? Or are you worried about protecting your skin?'

Seeing her master no more dismayed than he was raised the young woman's spirits, and she replied that she was perfectly capable of binding switches, but she could do no better with bands the likes of these.

'In that case you'd best get some decent bands,' old Ingmar replied, feeling in his finest Christmas spirit.

He left the main room, stepping over the other housemaid in the doorway with her scrubbing bucket, and halted as he stepped out onto the stone slab outside the door to consider whom he might ask to make a foray to the birch grove to gather some thin bands. The farmhands were still fully occupied with the Christmas firewood, his son was just coming down from the attic with the Christmas straw in his arms, and both his sons-in-law were busy moving all the farm equipment into the barn to make the yard presentable for Christmas. None of them had time to leave the farm.

And so the old man made up his mind quite placidly to undertake the task himself. He crossed the yard diagonally, as if heading for the cowshed, looked around to be sure no one was watching, and then slipped behind the wall of the barn where there ran a fairly well-trodden path up toward the woods. He did not consider it necessary to tell anyone where he was going, knowing full well that his son or one of his sons-in-law might prevail upon him to remain at home. And older people do prefer to have things their own way.

Following the path across the fields and through the cluster of little pines he eventually reached the birch grove. He left the path there and waded through the snow in search of a couple of saplings.

At about that same time, the wind was finally ready to let loose what it had been preparing for all day. It tore the snow out of the clouds and began to sweep across the woods with a long train of snowflakes in its wake.

Ingmar Ingmarsson had just leaned toward the ground to cut away a sapling when the wind caught him with its full charge of snow. As the old man straightened up, the wind let out a gust which blew a massive load of snowflakes into his face. His eyes filled with snow, and the wind whirled with such force that he spun around several times.

Probably the real explanation for the whole misfortune lay in the fact that Ingmar Ingmarsson was now an old man. In his youth probably no snowstorm would have made him dizzy. But now the world was twirling around him as it might have when he got carried away in a Christmas dance. The result was that, although he thought he was turning toward home, he was actually heading in precisely the opposite direction. He stepped straight into the huge pine forest that began just behind the birch grove instead of turning back toward the fields.

Darkness was falling fast, and among the smaller trees at the edge of the forest the sudden storm went on howling and whirling around him. The old man surely noted that he was walking among evergreens now, but without realizing that he was going the wrong direction, because there were also pines on the side of the birches bordering the farmland. Some time later he found himself so deep in the forest that the wind stilled. He was no longer aware of the storm, and the trees around him were both tall and wide. That was when he knew he had gone the wrong way and wanted to turn back.

The very idea that he could be lost made him dizzy and confused, and standing there deep in the pathless woods his head refused to clear enough for him to determine which way he ought to turn. He began by walking one direction, then another. Finally it occurred to him that he could retrace his own footsteps, but soon darkness had fallen and that, too, became impossible. And the trees around him just seemed taller and taller. He had to keep walking, he knew that, but he also realized he was moving farther and farther from the edge of the woods.

It was as if nothing could go right, everything seemed cursed, he felt doomed to wander through the forest all evening and arrive home too late for his Christmas bath.

He tried turning his cap around and retying his garters, but nothing reduced his confusion. It was pitch dark now and he began to think he would have to spend the night in the woods.

He leaned up against the trunk of an evergreen and stood still to sort out his thoughts. He was very much at home in these woods, had walked them so often that he ought to know every single tree. He had walked here as a young shepherd with his flock. He had walked here setting traps for wild birds. In his youth he had been a lumberjack here. He had seen felled trees lying beside their stumps and watched the woods grow up again.

Finally he thought he had begun to get some sense of where he was, and that all he had to do was to walk first one way and then another and he would find his way back. But no matter which way he went, he could tell he kept finding himself deeper and deeper in the woods.

At one point he felt his feet land on firm smooth ground and realized that he had finally hit on a road. He tried to follow it, because surely a road would lead somewhere. But that road led to a clearing at the edge of the woods, by which point the snowstorm was in full force, the path had vanished and there was nothing but drifts and deep snow. His courage began to fail him then, and he felt like a poor, pathetic soul fated to die in the wilderness.

He was becoming fatigued from dragging himself through the snow and sat down time after time on a rock to rest. But the moment he sat down he would feel himself falling asleep, and he knew that if he slept he would freeze to death. So he did his utmost to keep walking. That was the only way for him to save himself.

But as he walked on he was increasingly unable to resist the urge to sit down. He kept thinking that if only he could get some rest it wouldn't much matter to him if it cost him his life.

He experienced such pleasure from sitting still that the thought of death did not at all torment him. He took some pleasure in thinking about how, when he was dead, he would be eulogized at length in church. He remembered the fine exposition the old minister had presented of the life of his father and felt certain that kind words would be said about himself as well. He would be described as the owner of the very first farmstead in their community, and the great honor of being descended from such a distinguished lineage would be mentioned. As well as the responsibility it carried.

And of course there was a great deal of responsibility. He had always known that if you were an Ingmarsson you had to hold out to the bitter end.

Thus it shot through him like a shock that it would be less than honorable for him to be found frozen to death up in the wild woods. He did not want that to be part of his eulogy. So he stood up and walked on. He had been sitting for so long that a huge amount of snow fell from his fur coat when he set off.

But just a short while later he found himself sitting back down dreaming.

The idea of death was more and more appealing to him. He thought through his entire funeral and all the esteem that would be granted him once he was gone.

He imagined the huge feast set out in the upstairs banquet room, with the minister and his wife at the head of the table, and the judge there as well with a starched white napkin spread across his narrow chest, and the major's wife, proud in her black satin with that thick gold chain doubled and tripled around her neck.

He could see all the banquet rooms draped in white, the windows covered with white sheets and white fabric laid over the furniture. The road was covered in pine boughs all the way from the front steps to the church.

Baking and butchering and brewing and laundering for the

fortnight prior to the funeral. One hundred and eighty feet of firewood burnt in just two weeks' time.

The body lying in state in the inner chamber, a bit smoky in the seldom-heated rooms. Hymns sung by the coffin as the top was screwed on, silver plates attached. The entire farm swarming with guests.

All the village at work preparing the feast, all the high hats well-brushed, all the schnapps made last autumn consumed at the banquet, all the roads teeming with people, as if on their way to market.

Once again the old man rose to his feet. He had heard their voices, going on about him at the funeral feast.

'But how could he have gone and frozen to death that way?' asked the judge. 'Whatever was he doing up in the deep woods?'

And the captain answered that it was undoubtedly an effect of all the Christmas beer and schnapps.

This woke him once more. The Ingmarsssons were a family of moderate drinkers. No one was going to say of him that he had been under the influence when his time came. He began to walk and walk again. However, he was so tired that he could barely hold himself upright. He was high up in the woods now, he could tell, because the ground was rougher and rockier than down below. One foot got caught between some stones and he had trouble extracting it. He stood there moaning and groaning. He was nearly done for.

A moment later he tripped over a big pile of branches and had a soft fall, landing on the snow-covered tree limbs, so although he was not injured he was simply unable to pull himself back up. He wanted nothing more than to lie down and sleep. He shifted the branches aside a bit and crept down under them as if they were a fur rug. And when he crawled under those branches he suddenly felt the presence of something soft and warm. 'I do believe there's a bear hibernating in here,' he thought.

Then he felt the beast move and heard it sniff the air. He just went on lying there, perfectly still. His only thought was that he might as well let the bear eat him up. He was unable to walk a single step to escape.

The bear, however, didn't seem bothered by whatever was

seeking shelter under his roof on such a stormy night.

He just moved a bit deeper down into his den as if to make room for his guest, and very soon he was sound asleep, breathing quietly and evenly.

*

Meanwhile, very little Christmas peace had descended upon the venerable farm of the Ingmarssons. The entire evening of that Christmas Eve was spent searching for Ingmar Ingmarsson.

To begin with they looked all over the whole farmhouse and through all the outbuildings. They hunted from attic to cellar. Then they went to all the neighboring farms asking about the whereabouts of Ingmar Ingmarsson.

Having thus failed to find him, his sons and sons-in-law began searching the nearby fields and the farmland. The torches that should have lit their way to church the next morning were ignited and carried out into the wild snowstorm as they hunted for him on the roads and paths. But the wind had erased all traces of him, and its howling masked all human voices when they tried to shout his name. They were out and about until well past midnight, when it became clear to them that they would have to await daylight if they were to find the missing man.

In the earliest light of day everyone from the Ingmarsson farm was up, and all the men were waiting in the farmyard, ready to head out into the woods. However, before they left, the old mistress of the house came out and invited them all into the main room. She asked them to take seats on the benches lining the walls and she sat down at the Christmas buffet table with the Bible in front of her and began to read. First she located the passage she and her old eyes had in mind, a passage that might be suitable under such circumstances. She then commenced upon the parable of a certain man who went down from Jerusalem to Jericho and fell among thieves. She read slowly in a sing-song voice about this man in distress who was aided by the Samaritan. Her sons and sons-in-law, daughters and granddaughters sat around her on the benches. They were all similar in appearance to her and to each other, large and heavy, with unattractive features, though looking wise for their ages, because they were all of the ancient Ingmarsson lineage. They had reddish hair, freckled skin, and light blue eyes with fair eyelashes. Although each of them had his or her own features, they all had a stern cast to their mouths, heavy eyes, and slow movements, as if everything were an effort. And yet it was also clear that each of them was one of the foremost members of the community, and that they all knew themselves to be superior to others.

All the Ingmarsson sons and daughters released audible sighs throughout the Bible reading, wondering whether some Samaritan had found the head of their household and looked after him. Each member of the Ingmarsson clan felt as if they had lost part of their own soul any time a member of the family suffered a misfortune.

The old woman read and read until she arrived at the question: 'Which now of these three, thinkest thou, was neighbor unto him that fell among the thieves?' But before she was able to read the answer, the door opened from the outside and old Ingmar entered the room.

'Mother! Father is here,' one of the daughters said, and so they never heard that the one who had taken mercy upon the man was his neighbor.

*

Some time later that same day, the family matriarch again found herself in the same seat, reading her Bible. She was alone, the women having gone to church and the men out bear hunting in the woods. As soon as Ingmar Ingmarsson had had something to eat and drink he had headed out into the woods with his sons. For the fact is that it is man's duty to kill a bear, whenever and wherever he should encounter one. It was inconceivable to spare the life of a bear, because sooner or later that bear will have a taste for flesh, and will then not let anyone, neither animal nor human being, live.

But after their departure for the hunt, the mistress of the household experienced deep anxiety and sat down to read. This time she settled into the text that was the subject of that day's sermon, but she got no farther than to this: 'Peace on earth and goodwill to all men!' She just sat there staring at these words with her heavy gaze, and now and then heaving a deep sigh. She read no more, but repeated time after time in her slow, lugubrious voice:

'Peace on earth and goodwill to all men!'

Her eldest son entered the farmhouse just as she was inching her way through those words once more.

'Mother,' he said very softly.

She heard him, but did not lift her eyes from the book, merely asked:

'Are you not in the woods with the others?'

'Oh yes,' he said, even more softly, 'I was there with them.'

'Come here then, to the table,' she said, 'so I can see you!'

He approached, and when her gaze fell upon him, she saw him trembling. He had to grasp the edge of the table to settle his hands.

'Did you kill the bear?' she went on. Now he was unable to answer her in words; all he could do was shake his head.

The old woman looked up and did something she had not done since her son was a baby. She went to him, lay a caressing hand on his arm, stroked his cheek, and pulled him to her on the bench. Sitting beside him, she held his hand in hers.

'Now you tell me what happened, my lad!'

The man recognized this caress as having comforted him in his childhood when he was unhappy and helpless. He found it so moving that he began to cry.

'I can tell something must have happened to Father,' she said.

'Indeed, but it is worse still,' he wept.

'Is it worse still?'

The man was sobbing harder and harder, he could not imagine how he might gain control over his voice. In the end, he raised his coarse hand with its wide fingers and pointed to the phrase she had just been reading: 'Peace on earth.'

'Is it something about that?' she asked.

'Yes,' he answered.

'Is it something about Christmas peace?'

'Yes.'

'You were planning to commit an evil deed this morning?'

'Yes.'

'And God has punished us?'

'God has punished us.'

At last she was told what had happened. They had found their way to the bear's den, and when they were so close that the pile of branches was in sight, they stopped to ready their rifles. But before they were finished, the bear came rushing out of hibernation and straight at them. He looked neither right nor left but went directly for old Ingmar Ingmarsson and batted him over the brow so that he dropped to the ground as if struck by lightning. None of the others was attacked by the bear, who merely darted past the men and ran off through the woods.

*

That afternoon Ingmar Ingmarssson's wife and son went to the parsonage to report the death. His son did the speaking. The old mistress of the house sat listening, with a face as inert as if it were hewn in stone.

The minister sat in his armchair over by the desk. He had already taken out the ledger and recorded the death. He proceeded methodically, wanting to give himself a moment to consider his words to the widow and her son because this was, after all, something of an unusual case. The son had made an open account of all that had transpired, but the minister would have liked to know how the two of them were bearing up. The Ingmarssons were something of an enigmatic family.

When the minister closed the ledger, Ingmar Ingmarssson's son said:

'We also wanted to inform you, Sir, of our request that you not eulogize Father.'

The minister shifted his glasses to the top of his head and looked in the direction of the old woman, sharply and inquiringly. She remained sitting just as still as she had been. All she did was give the handkerchief she was holding between her hands a little twist.

'We'd like to have the funeral on a weekday,' the son continued.

'I see, I see,' said the minister.

His thoughts began to spin. So old Ingmar Ingmarsson would be laid to rest without anyone knowing. The congregation would not be standing on the church embankment watching the pallbearers carry the coffin to the grave.

'Neither will we be hosting a funeral banquet in his memory. We have already notified the neighbors that there will be no need to contribute to the preparation of the meal.'

'I see, I see,' the minister repeated, unable to think of anything else to say. He knew very well what it meant to the people of his parish to refrain from a funeral feast. He had seen what comfort it brought both to widows and those who lost their fathers to hold a worthy funeral banquet.

'There will be no funeral procession beyond my brothers and myself.'

The minister turned his pleading gaze toward the widow. Was she really going to agree to all this? He wondered whether Ingmar Ingmarsssson's son was really expressing her desires as well. She just sat there allowing herself to be deprived of all that must have been worth more to her than silver and gold.

'We'll have no ringing of the bells nor any silver plates on the coffin. This is what we want, Mother and I, but we have brought it up with you, Sir, to inquire whether you feel that we are being unfair to Father.'

And now the old woman spoke as well.

'In fact, what we want to know is whether you, Sir, are inclined to think that we are being unfair to Father.'

The minister continued to keep his counsel, so the old woman went on, more anxiously:

'I'd like you to know, Sir, that had my husband violated royal ordinances or the law, or had I had to cut him down from the gallows, I would still have given him a proper funeral like the one held for his father before him, being that the Ingmarssons fear no one, nor is there anyone to whom they must bow down. But at Christmas God has decreed peace between the animal kingdom and mankind, and that poor beast followed

God's commandment, but we broke it, and are therefore being punished by the Lord. And we are thus not in any position to feast and make merry.'

The minister rose and moved toward the old woman.

'What you are saying is accurate,' he said, 'and you must do as you see fit. And he added emphatically, though perhaps mostly to himself: 'The Ingmarssons are a formidable family.'

The old woman sat up a bit straighter at those words. The minister saw her for a moment as a symbol of the entire lineage. He could see what had endowed these sluggish and taciturn people with the power to become the leaders of the entire parish.

'It is incumbent upon the Ingmarssons to be a good model for the people,' she said. 'It is incumbent upon us to demonstrate our humility before the Lord.'

(From *Osynliga länkar*, 1909.)

THE CHANGELING

Bortbytingen

Translated by Peter Graves

A troll* wife came walking through the forest with her child in a birchbark basket on her back. The child was big and ugly, with hair like bristles, razor-sharp teeth and a claw on his little finger, but the troll wife, of course, thought that there couldn't possibly be a more beautiful child.

After a while she came to a place where the forest opened out a little. There was a road there, rutted and slippery with the roots of trees, and along it a farmer and his wife were riding.

The moment the troll wife caught sight of them, she wanted to slip back into the forest so as not to be seen by human beings, but then she noticed that the farmer's wife was carrying a child in her arms and that made her change her mind. 'I must see if a human child can possibly be as beautiful as my child,' she thought as she crouched down behind a big hazel bush close beside the road.

But as they were riding past, she became so eager that she peeked out far enough for the horses to catch sight of her big, black troll's head. They reared up and set off at full speed, very nearly causing the farmer and his wife to be thrown from their saddles. They called out in fright, leant forward to grasp the reins and the next moment were out of sight.

The troll wife, who had scarcely managed to catch a glimpse of the child, uttered a cry of vexation. But a moment later she was happy again, for there was the child lying on the ground at her feet.

The child had fallen from its mother's arms when the horses reared up but, by good fortune, landed quite unharmed in a pile of dry leaves. Frightened by the fall, it was now yelling loudly until the troll wife leaned over it when, both surprised and amused, it abruptly fell silent and reached out to pull on her black beard.

The troll wife stared at the human child in utter amazement. She looked at its slim fingers with their pink nails, at its clear blue eyes and at its little red mouth. She felt the softness of its hair, stroked its cheek with her hand and her amazement grew and grew. She just couldn't understand how a child could be so pink and soft and delicate.

Then, in a trice, the troll wife took the birch basket from her back, lifted out her own child and placed it beside the human child. When she saw what a difference there was between them, she began to bawl uncontrollably.

In the meantime, the farmer and his wife had regained control of their horses and were now returning to look for their child. The troll wife heard them approaching, but as she hadn't yet had her fill of gazing at the human child, she remained sitting beside it until the riders were almost in sight. Then she came to a quick decision: leaving her own child lying by the side of the road, she put the human child into the birch basket, slung it on her back and ran into the forest.

She was scarcely out of sight before the riders came into view. They were grand farming folk, the rich and respected owners of a large farm in the fertile valley at the foot of the hill. They had already been married for many years, but they only had this one child and it's easy to imagine how eager they were to get it back.

The farmer's wife was riding a couple of horse lengths in front of her husband and so was the first to catch sight of the child lying at the side of the road. It was yelling at the top of its voice to call its mother back and given the dreadful howling the woman must surely have realised the kind of child it was, but she was so anxious that the fall had killed her little one that her only thought was: 'Praise the Lord, he's alive!' Then she shouted to her husband, 'Our child is over here!' as she slid down from the saddle and hurried over to the troll child.

When the farmer got there, his wife was sitting on the ground looking as if she couldn't believe her own senses.

'My child didn't have teeth like awls,' she said, turning the child this way and that. 'My child didn't have hair like pig's bristle,' she wailed, her voice filled with more and more horror. 'My child didn't have a claw on his little finger.'

The farmer, certain that his wife had gone out of her mind, leapt quickly off his horse.

'Just look at the child and tell me if you can understand why he looks so strange!' she said, handing the child to her husband. He took the child from her, but the instant he looked at it he spat three times and tossed the child aside.

'This isn't our child,' he said, 'It must belong to a troll!'

His wife was still sitting at the edge of the road. She wasn't a quick thinker and she simply could not come up with an explanation for what had happened.

'What are you going to do with the child?' she exclaimed.

'Can't you see it's a changeling?' her husband asked. 'The trolls took their chance when our horses bolted. They stole our child and left one of their own in its place.'

'Where is my child now, then?' the farmer's wife asked.

'Away with the trolls, that's where it is,' her husband said.

Now his wife recognised the scale of their misfortune. She went as pale as a woman on her deathbed and her husband thought she was about to give up the ghost on the spot.

'Our child can't be that far away, can he?' he said, trying to calm her. 'We'll go into the forest and search.'

He tethered his horse to a tree and set off into the undergrowth. His wife rose to follow him, but then she noticed that the troll child was lying where he could easily be kicked by the horses, which were jumpy and uneasy at having him close to them. She shuddered at the very thought of touching the changeling, but still she moved him a little to the side so the horses couldn't reach him.

'Here's the rattle our boy was carrying when you dropped him,' the farmer called from the forest. 'Now I know I'm on the right track.' His wife hurried after him and they spent a long time searching in the forest. But they could find neither the child nor the troll, and when dusk began to fall, they had to return to their horses.

The farmer's wife wept and wrung her hands, whereas her husband went around with his jaw clenched, not saying a word to comfort her. He came from an old and good family that would have died out if he hadn't had a son. Now he was angry with his wife for having dropped their child to the ground. 'Whatever else, she ought to have hung on to the child,' he thought. But when he saw how distressed she was, he didn't have the heart to reproach her.

He had already helped her up into the saddle when she remembered the changeling.

'What shall we do about the troll boy?' she said.

'Where's he gone?' her husband wondered.

'He's over there under the bush.'

'Well, he's fine there,' her husband said with a bitter laugh.

'But we have to take him with us – we can't just leave him out here in the woods.'

'Oh yes we can,' the farmer said, putting his foot in the stirrup.

The farmer's wife thought her husband was right. They didn't actually need to take on the troll's child and she let her horse move a few steps. Then, all of a sudden, she found it impossible to ride on.

'It is a child after all,' she said. 'I can't just leave it here as food for the wolves. You must give me the boy.'

'I certainly won't,' her husband answered. 'He's fine lying there where he is.'

'If you don't give him to me now, I just know I shall have to come back here to fetch him tonight,' she said.

'It's not enough, then, for the trolls to steal my child – it looks as if they've warped my wife's mind as well,' the farmer muttered. Nevertheless, his love for her was so great he was used to doing everything the way she wanted, so he picked up the child and passed it to her.

By the following day the whole parish knew of their misfortune and all the sensible and experienced people hurried to the farm to offer wise counsel and warnings.

'Anyone who takes a changeling into their house should beat him with a rough stick,' one old woman said.

'Why should anyone treat him so harshly?' the farmer's wife asked. 'Ugly he may be, but he hasn't done anything wrong, has he?'

'Well, if you whip the troll child until his blood flows, the troll wife will come fast as she can, throw your own child back to you and take her own. I know many people who've got their children back that way.'

'Yes, but those children did not stay alive for long,' one of the old folk added, and the farmer's wife thought to herself that a method of that kind was of no use to her.

Towards evening, after she had been alone in the house with the changeling for a while, she started longing so passionately for her own child that she didn't know what she should do. 'Perhaps I should just do as I've been advised', she thought, but she could not bring herself to do it.

Just then the farmer came into the house. He had a stick in his hand and he asked for the changeling. His wife realised that he was intending to follow the advice of the wise women and beat the troll child in order to get his own child back. 'It's just as well for him to do it,' she thought. 'I'm so stupid, I could never bring myself to hit an innocent child.'

But no sooner had her husband struck the troll child once than she rushed over and grabbed his arm.

'No, don't hit him! Don't!' she begged.

'You do want your own child back, don't you?' her husband said, trying to pull his arm free.

'Of course I want him back,' his wife said, 'but not this way.'

The farmer raised his arm to strike another blow, but before it landed, his wife had thrown herself over the child so that the blow struck her.

'God in Heaven!' her husband said. 'I can see now that you are prepared to leave our child with the trolls for the whole of his life.'

He stood there waiting, but his wife remained lying in front of him, protecting the child. So he threw the stick aside and left the house, angry and distressed. Later he wondered why he hadn't done what he'd intended to do in spite of his wife's resistance, but there was something about her that overruled him. He couldn't go against her.

A few more days passed, days of sorrow and misery. It can be hard enough for a mother to lose her child, but to have it replaced by a changeling is the worst thing in the world. It keeps her longing perpetually alive and never allows it to be at rest.

'I don't know what I should give the changeling to eat,' she said to her husband one morning. 'He won't eat what I put in front of him.'

'That's hardly strange,' her husband said. 'Haven't you heard that trolls eat nothing but frogs and mice?'

'You can't really be asking me to go out to the frog pond to collect food for him, can you?' his wife said.

'No, I wouldn't ask any such thing,' her husband said. 'I think the best thing would be for him to starve to death.'

The whole week passed without the farmer's wife being able to get the troll to eat anything. She surrounded him with every good thing possible, but the troll child just whined and spat whenever she tried to get him to taste these delicacies.

One evening when it looked as if the boy was on the point of dying of hunger, the cat came dashing into the room with a rat in its mouth. The farmer's wife snatched the rat from the cat, threw it across to the changeling and hastily left the room to avoid seeing the troll child eating it.

But when the farmer noticed that his wife had actually started to collect frogs and spiders for the changeling, he felt such disgust for her that he couldn't conceal it any longer. He found it impossible to say a kind word to her but, for all that, she still retained so much of her old power over him that he didn't leave home.

As if that weren't enough, the servants, too, began to be disobedient and disrespectful to their mistress. Her husband pretended not to notice it and his wife came to realise that if she continued standing up for the changeling, she would have a hard time and face difficulties every single day God sent. But she was the sort of person who, if there was someone everyone hated, she would strive her utmost to come to the aid of the poor soul. And the more she suffered for the sake of the changeling, the more steadfastly she watched that no harm should befall him.

Several years passed and the farmer's wife was alone in the house one morning, sewing patch after patch on the child's clothing. 'Goodness me,' she thought as she sewed. 'There are no good days when you have to spend your time looking after a stranger's child.'

She sewed and sewed, but the holes were so big and there were so many of them that tears came to her eyes at the sight of them. 'I do know one thing, though,' she thought, 'if it was my own son's clothes I was having to mend, I wouldn't be counting the holes.'

'I'm having a hard time with this changeling,' the farmer's wife thought, on catching sight of yet another hole. 'Maybe the best thing would be to take him so far out into the forest that he couldn't find his way home and leave him there.'

'The truth is I wouldn't actually need to go to much trouble to be rid of him,' she thought after a while. 'If I let him out of my sight for a moment, he would drown in the well or burn himself in the stove or get bitten by the dog or kicked by the horses. In fact, it would be easy enough to be rid of him, given how naughty and foolhardy he is. There's no one on the farm who doesn't hate him and if I didn't keep him close to me the whole time, someone would quickly take the opportunity to get rid of him.'

She went over to look at the child who was lying asleep in a corner of the house. He had grown and he was even more ugly than when she saw him for the first time. His mouth had grown into a snout, his eyebrows were like two stiff brushes and his skin was completely brown.

'Mending your clothes and caring for you may perhaps be acceptable, but that's the least I have to put up with for your sake,' she thought. 'My husband has become so unpleasant to me, the farmhands scorn me, the maids laugh at me, the cat spits when he sees me, the dog growls and bares his teeth, and it's all your fault.'

'I could put up with animals and people hating me – I could put up with that,' she exclaimed. 'The worst thing is that every time I see you, I long more than ever for my own child. Oh, my sweet child, where are you? Do you have to make your bed and sleep on moss and brushwood, there with that troll wife?'

The door opened and the farmer's wife went quickly back to her sewing. Her husband came in. He was looking happy and he spoke to her in a more friendly way than he'd done for a long time.

'It's market day today over at the church village,' he said. 'What do you say to us going there?'

His wife was pleased at the suggestion and said she would really like that.

'Get ready as quickly as you can,' her husband said. 'We'll need to go on foot as the horses are out working in the fields. But if we take the road over the hill, we'll be there in time.'

A little while later the farmer's wife stood waiting at the door, dressed in her best clothes, clean, tidy and smart. This was the nicest thing that had happened to her for many years and she'd completely forgotten the troll child. 'But,' the thought occurred to her suddenly, 'perhaps my husband just wants to get me away so the farmhands can kill the changeling while I'm out.' She went quickly into the house and came back with the troll child in her arms.

'Can't you leave that thing at home?' her husband said, but he spoke in a mild voice with no trace of anger.

'No, I can't risk leaving him,' she answered.

'Well, it's up to you,' the farmer said. 'But it will be difficult for you, carrying a burden like him over the hill.'

So they set off and, being a steep uphill walk, it was hard going. They had to climb all the way to the top of the hill before the road eased off towards the church.

In the end the farmer's wife grew so tired she scarcely had the strength to go on. Time after time she tried to encourage the big boy to walk himself, but he wouldn't.

Her husband was quite happy and was more friendly than he'd been since they lost their own child.

'Give me the changeling, now,' he said. 'I'll carry him for a while.'

'Oh no, I can manage well enough,' his wife said. 'I don't want you burdened with the awful troll.'

'Why should you have to struggle with it on your own?' he said, taking the boy from her.

Just at the point where the farmer took the child, the road was at its most difficult. It was smooth and slippery as it ran along the edge of a steep ravine, and it was so narrow that there was barely room to put one foot in front of the other. The farmer's wife was walking behind him and she was suddenly overcome with fear that something might happen to her husband given that he was struggling with the weight of the child.

'Go slowly here!' she called, convinced he was walking far too quickly and carelessly. And a moment later, he did trip and came very close to dropping the child into the abyss.

'If the child fell, we'd be rid of it for ever,' she thought. But at that same moment she realised that her husband actually was intending to drop the child off the cliff and to pretend it happened by accident.

'Ah, now I see,' she thought, 'so that's how it is. He's set all this up to get rid of the changeling without me seeing it was done on purpose. Well, I suppose it might be best if I let him do as he pleases.'

Once again the farmer stumbled on a stone and once again the changeling came close to slipping from his arms.

'Give me the child! You're going to fall and drop it,' his wife said.

'No!' her husband replied. 'I really will be careful.'

And at that moment he tripped for the third time. He let go of the child and reached out to grab the branch of a tree. His wife was walking close behind him and, although she had only just said to herself that it would be good to be rid of the changeling, she now threw herself forward, caught the edge of the troll boy's clothing and pulled him back on to the road.

Her husband turned round to her. His face had changed completely and taken on an ugly look.

'You weren't so quick off the mark when you dropped our child in the forest,' he said angrily.

His wife did not answer. She was so distressed that her husband's kindness had been nothing but pretence that she began to cry.

'Why are you crying?' he said harshly. 'It wouldn't have been any great misfortune if I'd let the urchin fall. Come on now, otherwise we'll be too late.'

'I don't think I've got any desire to go to the market now,' she said.

'Oh well, I've lost any desire to go there, too,' her husband said, agreeing with her.

As he walked home, he found himself wondering how much longer he could put up with his wife. If he were to use his strength and tear the child away from her, everything between them could be good again, he thought. He was on the point of starting to struggle with her for the child when he met her eyes resting sadly and anxiously on him. So for her sake he controlled himself once again and everything remained as before.

Several more years passed and then one summer's night their farm went up in flames. When everyone woke, the house and its rooms were full of smoke and the whole loft was a sea of flame. All thoughts of putting it out or of saving anything were out of the question, the only thing to do was to hurry out so as not to perish in the fire.

Once the farmer was outside in the yard, he stood and watched his burning house.

'There's just one thing I really want to know,' he said, 'and that is who brought this misfortune down on me.'

'Who else could it possibly be than that changeling,' a farmhand said, 'he's forever collecting sticks and straw and setting them alight indoors and out.'

'And yesterday he carried a pile of dry twigs up into the loft and was about to set light to them when I saw him,' a maid said.

'He probably lit it late last night instead,' the farmhand said. 'You can be sure that he's the one you can thank for the whole catastrophe.'

'If only he'd burned up with it, I wouldn't have any complaints about my old home going up in flames,' the farmer said.

As he was saying this, his wife came out of the house dragging the child behind her. The farmer rushed over to her, snatched the changeling, lifted him aloft and threw him back into the house.

At that point the fire was raging and roaring up through the roof and out of the windows, and the heat was horrendous. For one moment, pale with horror, his wife stared at her husband, before turning and rushing into the house after the child,

'You can burn up too, as far as I'm concerned,' her husband shouted after her.

But she came back out and she had the changeling with her. Her hands were badly scorched and almost all her hair was burnt away. No one said a word to her when she came out. She went over to the well, doused some sparks on the folds of her skirt and then sat down with her back to the well head. The troll child lay in her lap and soon went to sleep, but she stayed there, sitting upright and awake and gazing sadly in front of her. A whole crowd of people hurried past her towards the burning house, but no one spoke to her. They all seemed to find her so strange and frightening that they didn't dare come near her.

At daybreak, with the house burnt to the ground, her husband approached her.

'I can't put up with this any longer,' he said. 'I know you know I'm unwilling to leave you, but I don't want to live with a troll any longer. I'm leaving now and I shall never return.'

When his wife heard these words and saw her husband turn and walk away, she felt it tear at her innermost being. She wanted to hurry after him, but the weight of the troll child lay heavy in her lap. She remained sitting there, knowing that she lacked the strength to free herself.

The farmer set off straight into the forest, thinking to himself that this would likely be the last time he took this road. He'd walked no more than a short way up the hill when a little lad came running towards him. He was as slim and handsome as a sapling, with hair soft as silk and eyes that shone like steel.

'Oh what misery! That's exactly how my son would have looked if I'd been allowed to keep him,' the farmer said. 'What an heir I'd have had! How different from that swarthy good-for-nothing my wife brought back to the farm.'

'Good day to you, forest-goer!' the farmer greeted him. 'And where are you off to?'

'And good day to you!' the child said. 'If you can guess who I am, then you'll soon guess where I'm going.'

When the farmer heard the voice, the colour drained from his face.

'The way you speak is the way my people speak,' he said. 'If my own son wasn't with the trolls, I'd say that you are that son.'

'Well, you've guessed right, father,' the boy said with a laugh. 'And since you've guessed right, I'll tell you that I'm on my way to see my mother.'

'You shouldn't go and see your mother,' the farmer said. 'She doesn't ask after you and she doesn't ask after me. She has no room in her heart for anything apart from that big, swarthy troll boy.'

'So that's what you think, father, is it?' the boy said, looking deep into his father's eyes. 'Perhaps it would be best, then, if I were to stay with you for a start.'

The farmer was so overwhelmed with joy at meeting the boy that his eyes filled with tears.

'Oh yes, just stay with me!' he said, taking the boy in his arms and lifting him high in the air. He was so afraid that he would lose the boy again that he walked on carrying the boy in his arms.

After they had walked just a few steps, the boy began to talk to him.

'It's just as well that you're not carrying me as carelessly as you carried the changeling,' he said.

'What do you mean?' the farmer asked.

'Well, you see, the troll wife was walking along the other side of the ravine with me in her arms and every time you stumbled and came close to dropping the changeling, she came close to letting me fall.'

'Really? Are you telling me you were walking along the other side of the ravine?' the farmer spoke with cautious deliberation.

'I'd never ever been so frightened before,' the boy said. 'If you'd thrown the troll boy down into the ravine, the troll wife would have thrown me down after him. If mother hadn't …'

The farmer began to walk more slowly while trying to question the boy about everything.

'You must tell me what kind of time you have had among the trolls.'

'It could be hard at times,' the small boy said, 'but as long as mother was kind to the troll boy, the troll wife was kind to me.'

'Did she used to beat you?' the farmer asked.

'She didn't beat me any more often than you beat her child.'

'What were you given to eat?' his father went on.

'Every time mother gave the troll boy frogs and mice, I would get bread and butter. But when you put bread and meat in front of the troll boy, the troll wife would give me snakes and thistles. I almost died of starvation the first week. If mother hadn't then …'

When the child said this, the farmer turned right round and began walking quickly back down the valley.

'I don't know why or how,' he said, 'but I think there's a smell of smoke about you.'

'Well, there's nothing strange about that,' the child said. 'Last night, when you threw the troll child into the burning house, they threw me into the fire. If mother hadn't …'

The farmer now set off in such a hurry that he was almost running, but then he suddenly came to a halt.

'Now,' he said, 'now you must tell me what led the trolls to set you free.'

'When mother sacrificed something that was worth more than life to her, the trolls no longer had any power over me and let me go,' the boy said.

'Did she sacrifice something worth more than life to her?' the farmer asked.

'Indeed, she did. It was when she let you go in order to be able to keep the troll boy,' the child said.

The farmer's wife was still sitting in the same place by the well. She wasn't asleep, but she felt as if turned to stone. She was incapable of moving and saw as little of what was going on around her as if she really was dead. Then she heard her husband's voice calling her name from far away and her heart began beating again. Life returned and she opened her eyes and looked around, still no more than half-awake. It was bright day, the sun was shining and the lark was singing, and it seemed impossible that she would have to bear a burden of misfortune on such a beautiful day. But immediately thereafter she saw the charred beams that lay around her and all the people with blackened hands and sweating faces. She knew then that she was waking to a life even sadder than her old life had been, but she still sensed that her suffering was at an end. She looked around for the changeling. He wasn't in her lap and he was nowhere close by. If things had been as before, she would have leapt up and begun searching for him, but now she somehow felt it was unnecessary.

Once again she heard her husband calling to her from over by the forest. He was coming down the narrow path towards the farm and all the neighbours who had helped put the fire out ran towards him and surrounded him so that she couldn't see him. All she heard was him calling her name time after time, as if to make her hurry to meet him as the others were doing.

The voice bore a message of great joy, but she still remained sitting motionless. She didn't dare move. At last the crowd of people clustered around her and her husband stepped forward from among them, approached her and placed a beautiful child in her arms.

'Here is our son. He has come back to us,' her husband said, 'and it is you and no one else who saved him.'

(From *Troll och människor*, 1915.)

Note

79 *troll*: trolls frequently figured in Swedish folklore, particularly in southern and central Sweden. They lived in the forests, in the rocks, under the ground, but in many ways their lives parallelled the lives of humankind. Trolls were frequently blamed when things went wrong, when things disappeared, when the cattle were sick and so on. The belief

that they sometimes stole human children and left their own offspring in their place ('changelings') was not uncommon and would sometimes be used to explain away unusual or difficult behaviour in human children.

THE FIDDLER

Spelmannen

Translated by Linda Schenck

It can only be said of Lars Larsson the fiddler from Ullerud that in his later years he was a modest and humble fellow. However, people also say he wasn't always that way. In his younger years he was so arrogant and boastful that he drove folks to utter despair.

They say that something then transformed him and made a new man of him over a single night. This is the way it happened.

One Saturday night Lars Larsson was out walking, fiddle under his arm. He was in his brightest and most cheerful state of mind, returning as he was from festivities at which his music-making had drawn both old and young up onto the dance floor.

So he wandered along remembering how, for as long as his bow had been fiddling, not a soul had been able to sit or stand still. The village hall had been such a whirlwind of spinning and twirling it had seemed to him now and then as if the tables and chairs were at it as well.

'I do believe there's never been a fiddler the likes of me in these parts,' he said to himself.

'But I didn't have an easy time of it before I was as good as I am now,' he mused.

'It wasn't easy for me as a child when my mother and father sent me out to herd the goats and sheep and I lost track of everything else, just wanting to sit strumming my fiddle. Not to mention how back home they wouldn't even get me a proper instrument. I had nothing but a wooden box I'd stretched some strings across.

'I was all right in the woods during the day, but when I came home at night without my herd because I'd let the animals stray, it wasn't much fun. I don't know how many times I had to listen to my parents rebuke me, calling me a n'er-do-well and telling me I would never amount to anything.'

A little stream meandered close to where he was walking. The ground in the woods was rocky and uneven, and the stream had difficulty making its way. It twisted and turned in different directions, spilled down in little cascades, and still didn't seem to be getting anywhere. In contrast, the path the fiddler was following ran as straight and true as it could. Consequently, it kept bumping up against the stream, and at each crossing there was a little bridge. So the fiddler also had to cross the stream numerous times, and this gave him great pleasure. He felt like he had company on his way through the woods.

Where he walked, summer's night prevailed. Although it was not yet sunrise, the night was so bright it might as well have been.

Things weren't quite like daytime, however. The colors were completely different. The sky was utterly white. The trees and the thick undergrowth shimmered in hues of gray. And yet everything was just as clearly delineated as during the day, and when Lars Larsson was standing on one of the innumerable bridges looking down into the stream, he could make out each individual bubble that pearled its way up through the water.

'When I happen upon this kind of stream in the wild,' the fiddler thought, 'I can't help but reflect on my own life. I've been just as headstrong as the stream about forcing myself past every impediment that stood in my way. First there was Father: he stood up and opposed me like a solid rock. Then there was Mother: she tried to keep me calm, as if she were bedding me down in the moss. But I slipped past both Father and Mother and out into the world I went.

'Oh goodness gracious, I imagine Mother's still sitting back home weeping over me. But what do I care? She ought to have known I'd make something of myself, and not tried to stand in my way.'

Impatiently, he tore a handful of leaves from a bush and tossed them into the stream.

'Right, just like I tore myself away from everything back home,' he said, gazing as the water in the stream transported the leaves away.

'I wonder if Mother knows I'm the best fiddler in all of Värmland now?' he asked himself as he moved along.

He strode swiftly ahead until once more he came to the stream. There he stopped, staring down into the water once more.

At that spot the water was very turbulent and produced a tremendous din. To the fiddler's amazement when he stopped to listen, at night the noises from around the stream sounded very different than they would have during the day. There was no bird song from the treetops, nor was there the rustling of either pine needles or leaves. No carriage wheels were crunching on the road and no cowbells were tinkling in the woods. Nothing was rushing but the water in the stream, and for that reason its sounds were far more audible than during the day. It was as if every conceivable and inconceivable creature was raising a ruckus and making a great fuss down in the depths of the stream. It sounded first and foremost as if someone was sitting down there milling grain between huge stones, though at times there was a clanking as if drinking cups were toasting amicably, and at other times the noise was like the members of a congregation when they have left church after the sermon and gathered outside for a lively chat.

'This is its own kind of music,' the fiddler mused, 'but I find it difficult to say there is anything very special about it. To my mind the tune I was composing just the other day merits listening to far better.'

Still, the longer Lars Larsson stood there listening to the turbulence of the stream, the better it came to sound to him.

'I believe you're picking up,' he said to the churning stream. 'I guess you've realized that the best fiddler in all of Värmland is standing here listening to you.'

The very second he said that he seemed to perceive out of

the depths a couple of clear, metallic tones rising, like someone plucking a string to hear if it is properly tuned.

'Aha, the Water Sprite* himself, present and accounted for! I can hear him starting to tune up his fiddle. All right then, let's hear if you can play better than me,' laughed Lars Larsson. 'But I can't stand around all night waiting for you to get started,' he shouted down toward the water after a few moments. 'I've got to move on, but I promise to stop at the next bridge, too, to see whether your music-making measures up to mine.'

He walked on, and as the stream turned deeper into the woods on its meandering way, he began to think once again of his home.

'I wonder how the little brook is doing, the one that runs through our farmyard. I'd love to see it again. I suppose I ought to go home and check on Mother, see whether she's impoverished now that Father has died. But busy man that I am, it's nigh on impossible. As I say, busy as I am, I can't really manage anything but my fiddle. Goodness, I'm barely free a single evening in any given week.'

In a short while he happened again upon the stream, at which point he began to wonder. At this bridge, the water wasn't rushing along in rolling rapids, it simply ran along quite peacefully. It looked very black, gleaming under the night-gray trees in the woods, bearing with it only occasional white, foamy tufts from the turbulent water upstream.

When the fiddler walked out onto the bridge and heard no other sound from the stream than a regular, gentle lapping, he began to laugh.

'I should have figured, Water Sprite, that you wouldn't bother to turn up for our meeting,' he called out. 'Although I've always heard you're a fine fiddler, you can't be much of one if you just lie down there in the stream and never hear the local gossip. I'll bet you realize that the man who is standing here is better informed than you, which would explain why you don't want to let me hear you play.'

And so he walked on, losing the stream from sight once more.

Now he came into a part of the woods he had always found

eerie and unwelcoming. The ground was rough with large rocks and gnarly upturned pine roots between them. If there was anything creepy or threatening in these woods, this is where you would expect it to be crouching.

When the fiddler started wending his way through the rocky patch, he shivered and began wondering whether it might have been unwise of him to boast as he had in the presence of the Water Sprite.

He imagined that the huge clumps of pine roots were making menacing gestures in his direction.

'You'd better take care after acting so superior to the Water Sprite,' they seemed to be indicating.

His heart tightened with anxiety. His entire chest felt weighted down, he could barely breathe, and his hands had gone icy cold. He stood in the middle of the path, trying to talk some sense into himself.

'Come on, there is no fiddler down in the stream,' he encouraged himself. 'That sort of thing is naught but superstition and old wives' tales. It doesn't matter a mite what I may have said or neglected to say to him.'

As he said this, he looked around the woods as if seeking confirmation that what he was saying was true. Had it been daytime, probably every single little leaf would have given him a wink, as if to say there were no dangers in the woods, but now, at night, all the trees stood there withdrawn into themselves and silent, looking for all the world as if they were concealing every possible kind of secret.

Lars Larsson grew increasingly frightened. The thing that terrified him most was the idea of having to cross yet another bridge over the stream before it and the path went their separate ways.

He wondered what the Water Sprite would do to him as he crossed that last bridge. Who knew, he might extend a big, black hand from the water and pull him down into the depths.

Having put himself into such a fright, he even considered turning back. But if he did he'd have to cross the stream again in any case. And if he were to deviate from the path and turn into the woods, surely he would inevitably happen upon it, what with its many twists and turns.

His anxiety was so great he hardly knew what to do with himself. He was captured and ambushed and tied up and bound by that stream, with no evident means of escape.

At last he saw the final bridge ahead. On the opposite bank in front of him, was an old mill that must have been abandoned many years ago. The huge millwheel hung immobile over the water, the sluicegate lay rotting on the bank of the stream, the raceways were overgrown with moss, and wall ferns and beard lichen filled the openings.

'If only everything had been as in the old days, and there were people there,' thought the fiddler, 'I would now be delivered beyond all peril.'

Still, he did feel comforted by the sight of a building created by human hands, and so he was barely frightened at all as he crossed the stream. Indeed, nothing terrible happened to him, either. It seemed the Water Sprite had no score to settle with him. The only thing that astonished him was that he had been walking along working himself up to a fright over nothing.

He began to feel quite pleased and safe, and this pleasure was further enhanced when the millhouse door opened and a young lass came toward him. She looked to be an ordinary farmgirl, with a cotton kerchief on her head, a short skirt and a loose blouse, and her feet were bare.

She approached the fiddler and said straight out:

'If you play for me, I'll dance for you.'

'Certainly,' said the fiddler, who was now in fine fettle as he no longer had anything to fear, 'I'll do that. It will be a pleasure. Never in my life have I refused to play for a pretty girl who wanted to dance.'

He stood up on a rock alongside the millpond, raised his fiddle to his chin and began to play.

The young woman took a few steps in time to the music, but then she stopped.

'What kind of a polska* is that you're playing?' she asked. 'There's no energy in it.'

The fiddler changed his tune, trying a dance that went a bit faster. The lass just stood there, not a bit more pleased.

'There's no way I can dance to such a dull polska,' she said
Lars Larsson took up the wildest polska he knew.

'If this one doesn't please you,' he said, 'you'll have to call in a
fiddler who's better than I am.'

The moment he said those words he felt a hand seize his arm
right at the elbow. It took control of the bow and helped him
pick up speed.

A tune poured forth from his fiddle the likes of which he had
never heard. The tempo was so fast he felt that not even a rolling
wheel could have kept up.

'Now that's what I call a polska to dance to,' said the lass as
she began to spin.

But the fiddler wasn't looking at her. The tune he was playing
astonished him so that he shut his eyes the better to hear it.

Some time later when he opened them the lass had vanished,
but he barely gave her a thought. He just went on playing for a
good long time simply because he'd never before heard a fiddler
sound like that.

'It's getting to be due time to wind this up,' he thought a
while later, wanting to lower his bow.

But the bow went on fiddling. He was unable to make it stop.
It went up and down across the strings tugging his hand and
arm right along. Neither could the hand that was holding his
fiddle and fingering the strings release its grip.

Lars Larsson broke out in a cold sweat and was really and
truly frightened.

'How will this ever end? Am I going to sit here playing until
doomsday comes?' he asked himself in desperation.

His bow just went on, rushing from one tune to the next as
if by magic. Time after time there were new melodies, one more
beautiful than the last, and the poor fiddler could not help but
become aware of the insignificance of his own music-making.
This was what pained him most, more than the fatigue.

'Whoever is playing my fiddle, he has mastered the art.
Whereas I, for all my life, have never been more than a bungler.
Not until now have I had the opportunity to learn what real
music-making is.'

Now and then, for an instant, he found himself so carried

away by the music that he forgot his unfortunate dilemma. But soon he would feel his arms aching with exhaustion and he would be seized once more with despair.

'I'll never be able to put my fiddle down until I have played myself to death. I see now that the Water Sprite will not be satisfied with less.'

He began to weep over his fate, still playing all the while.

'I would have been better off staying home with Mother in our little cottage. What was the point of all my distinction if it was to end this way?'

He sat there for hours on end. Morning came, the sun rose and the birds were chirping all around him. Still he went on playing and playing, endlessly.

As the dawning day was a Sunday, he remained sitting there by the old mill all alone. No one walked past on their way to the woods. All the people were going to church down in the dale, and in the villages along the main road.

The morning went on and the sun rose higher and higher. The birds grew still, but the long needles on the pine trees began to murmur.

Lars Larsson did not let the heat of the summer's day slow him down. He played and he played. Finally evening came, the sun sank, but his bow required no rest, and his arm went on moving.

'One thing is certain, this will be the death of me,' he said. 'And it is a just punishment for all my arrogance.'

Late that evening someone came through the woods. It was a poor old woman, back bent, gray haired and with a face careworn with great grief.

'How extraordinary,' thought the fiddler, 'I seem to recognize that old woman. Could it possibly be Mother? Could Mother have grown so old and gray?' He gave a shout to call himself to her attention.

'Mother, Mother, come over here to me,' he said.

She slowed down reluctantly.

'I can now hear with my own ears that you are the best fiddler in Värmland,' she said. 'I can understand, I suppose, why you cannot be bothered with an old woman like me.'

'Mother, Mother, don't pass me by!' he called out. 'I am no great fiddler, I'm naught but an unfortunate fellow. Come here and let me speak with you.'

His mother went closer and saw him sitting there playing. His face was as ashen as a corpse's, his hair dripping with perspiration, and blood was beginning to seep out from under his fingernails.

'Mother, my arrogance has brought me low, and now I'll have to play until I die. But before I do, will you tell me if you can forgive me for leaving you alone and in poverty in your old age?'

His mother was seized with great compassion for her son and all the anger she had felt vanished as if carried away on the wind.

'Of course I forgive you,' she said. And as if she saw his anguish and wanted him to be sure she meant what she said, she confirmed her forgiveness in the name of the Lord.

'In the name of God our Savior I forgive you,' she said.

And when she said these words his bow stopped moving, his fiddle fell to the ground, and the fiddler rose up, delivered and liberated. For the spell was broken, because his old mother had felt such compassion for him in his hour of need that she had uttered the name of God over him.

(From *En saga om en saga och andra sagor*, 1908.)

Notes

97 *Strömkarlen*, here The Water Sprite, also often referred to as *Näcken* or *Näck* in Swedish and The Nixie or Nix in English is a shapeshifting water spirit common in Germanic mythology and folklore.

99 *pols*ka: a Swedish folk tune played either to be listened to or danced to, in which case it is a dance for couples, often in three time, and can be played on many different instruments. In 2024, the polska was added to the Swedish list of terms denoting 'living heritage'. *Levande kulturarv* is the national website of the UNESCO Convention for the Safeguarding

of the Intangible Cultural Heritage in Sweden. See: https://
levandekulturarv.se/forteckningen/element/polska---musik-
och-dans

Epochs, Societies and Values

THE OUTLAWS

De fågelfrie

Translated by Peter Graves

A farmer murdered a monk and fled to the forest as an outlaw. There he met another outlaw already out in the wilds, a fisherman from the outermost skerries who'd been accused of stealing a herring net. The two of them joined forces, lived in a cave in the earth, set snares, made arrows, baked bread on a slab of granite and each guarded the life of the other. The farmer never left the forest but the fisherman, whose crime was less heinous than his, sometimes shouldered a load of the animals they'd hunted and slipped out among the local people. There he would be given milk and butter and arrowheads and clothes in exchange for black capercaillie and blue-sheened blackcock, for long-eared hares and delicate roedeer. This enabled the outlaws to survive.

The cave in which they lived was dug into the slope of a hill, its entrance protected by great slabs and spiky blackthorn. A bushy spruce tree grew on the roof and the chimney of the cave was in among its roots. The rising smoke filtered through the dense, thickly needled branches of the tree and disappeared imperceptibly into the air. When passing to and from their dwelling the men would wade in the forest burn that rose below the rocky slope. No one sought the tracks of the outlaws under its merry rippling water.

At first they were hunted like wild beasts. The farmers would gather as they did for bear or wolf drives. The forest would be surrounded by bowmen, while spearmen moved in and left no dark crannies or bushy thickets unsearched. As the hunt passed through the forest, the outlaws would lie in their dark cave panting in fear and listening breathlessly. The fisherman could put up with this all day long, but an intolerable dread drove the man who had committed murder out into the open where he could see his enemy. He was seen and hunted but this seemed to him sevenfold better than lying there in silence, powerless and inactive. He fled from his hunters, slid down precipices, leapt across torrents and scaled vertical walls of rock. The spur of danger summoned up all the strength and skill hidden in him. His body became as tight as a coiled spring, his foot did not slip nor his hand lose its grip, and his eyes and ears perceived everything twice as acutely as before. He understood the whisperings of the leaves and the warnings of the rocks. Climbing onto a bluff he turned to face his pursuers and hurled biting gibes at them in rhyme. When the spears whined and whistled, he caught them quick as lightning and sent them back down at his enemies. And as he crashed on through the branches that whipped him as he went, a voice within him sang a paean in praise of his progress.

An exposed rocky ridge ran through the forest and a towering pine stood solitary on its crest. Its reddish brown trunk was bare but up in its crown of dense swaying branches there was a hawks' nest. The courage of the fugitive became so reckless that he climbed up there while his pursuers sought him down on the wooded slopes. He sat in the treetop wringing the necks of the young hawks as the hunt moved on far below him. The male and female birds, intent upon revenge, dived at the thief. They flapped at his face, went for his eyes with their beaks, beat him with their wings and gouged bloody stripes across his weather-beaten face with their talons. He fought back, laughing. He stood upright beside the nest slashing at the birds with his sharp knife and, in the joy of the game, he forgot both peril and pursuers. When he found time to look for them they had moved off in another direction. It had not occurred to any of them to seek their prey up on the bare rock ridge. Not one of them had raised his eyes to the heights and seen this boyish bravado, the feats he was performing in a sleepwalker's daze while his life was in utter peril.

A shudder ran through the man once he saw his life was safe. He reached out for support with trembling hands and dizziness gripped him as he measured the height he had climbed. Groaning with the fear of falling, afraid of the birds, afraid of being seen, afraid of everything, he slid back down the trunk of the pine. He lay down on the rocks so as not to be seen and dragged himself across the slabs until the undergrowth covered him. He hid beneath the tangled branches of the young spruces and sank down, exhausted and helpless, on the moss. One man alone would have been enough to capture him.

*

The fisherman' s name was Tord. He was no more than sixteen years old but strong and brave. He had already been living in the forest for a year.

The farmer was called Berg and his by-name was Giant. He was the tallest and strongest man in the district and handsome and well-formed with it. His shoulders were broad, his waist slim, and his hands so elegant they looked as though they had never undertaken hard work. His hair was brown and his face fair-skinned. After living in the forest for a time everything about his appearance became more awesome. His gaze grew piercing, the muscles round his nose that caused his brows to furrow stood out thick as a finger, and his eyebrows grew bushy. The upper part of his forehead protruded beyond the lower part and became ever more prominent with the passing of time. His lips shut tighter than before, his whole face became leaner, the hollows at his temples becoming very deep and his massive jawbones standing out more clearly. His body lost its fullness but his muscles became knots of iron. His hair quickly went grey.

Young Tord never tired of looking at this man. Never before had he beheld anything so magnificent and so powerful. In Tord's mind Berg stood as tall as the forest and as mighty as the surf, and so he took him as his master and worshipped him as a god. It was quite natural for Tord to be the one to carry the hunting spear, to bear home the game, to fetch water and light the fire. Berg the Giant accepted his service but scarcely said a friendly word to him. He scorned him because he was a thief.

The outlaws did not live as robbers or footpads but supported themselves by hunting and fishing. If Berg the Giant hadn't murdered a holy man the farmers would soon have ceased pursuing him and left him in peace up among the hills. But, as it was, they feared some great misfortune would befall the district because a man who'd raised his hand against one of God's servants still roamed unpunished. When Tord went down to the valley with game, they offered him great wealth and forgiveness for his own crime if only he would show them the way to Berg the Giant's cave so they could take him prisoner while he slept. But the lad always refused, and if anyone attempted to follow him stealthily into the forest, he would lead them a false trail with such cunning that they abandoned the pursuit.

Berg asked Tord once whether the farmers ever tried to tempt him to betray him and when he heard the reward they offered he said scornfully that Tord was a fool not to take such an offer.

Tord looked up at him then with an expression that Berg the Giant had never seen before. No one, no beautiful woman in his youth nor even his wife and children, had looked at him that way. The look said: 'You are my lord, my chosen master. You may beat me and insult me as you wish, but I shall still remain faithful.'

Berg the Giant paid more attention to the boy after that and noticed that he was brave in deed but shy in speech. Death held no terror for him. When the lakes were newly frozen over, when the marshes were at their most dangerous in spring, when quagmires lurked beneath the abundant flowers of cotton grass and cloudberry, it was then that the boy took pleasure in crossing them. He seemed to feel a need to place himself in danger as if as a substitute for the storms and horrors of the sea he no longer had to face. But he was afraid in the forest at night, and even in the middle of the day the darkest thickets or the outstretched white roots of a fallen pine could frighten him. Yet he was too shy to have an answer when Berg the Giant asked him about these things.

Tord did not sleep on the raised bed of soft moss and warm hides close to the fire deep in the cave, but every night once Berg had gone to sleep Tord would creep out to the entrance and lie there on a slab of rock. Berg discovered this and, although he was well aware of the reason, he asked what it was supposed to mean. Tord did not explain it to him. To avoid more questions, he did not sleep in the doorway for two nights, but after that he returned to his post.

One night when the spindrift was whirling around the treetops and even finding its way into the densest and most storm-proof of the thickets, the spinning snowflakes penetrated the outlaws' cave. Tord, who was lying immediately inside the entrance they had closed up with stone slabs, found himself on a bed of melting drift snow when he woke in the morning. Some days later he fell ill. His lungs wheezed and he suffered excruciating pains when he filled them to take in air. He kept going as long as his strength lasted but one evening, when he bent down to blow the fire, he collapsed to the ground and stayed there.

Berg the Giant came to him and bade him take to his bed. Tord groaned with pain and lacked the strength to rise. Berg slid his arms under him and lifted him onto the bed. But such was his disgust at touching this wretched thief that he felt as if he had taken hold of a slimy serpent and his tongue tasted as if he had eaten unholy horse flesh.*

He covered the boy with his own great bearskin and gave him water. There was no more he could do. Nor did things take a serious turn and Tord soon recovered. But the fact that Berg had to perform Tord's tasks and be his servant brought them closer. And now, while Berg sat there in the cave in the evenings cutting shafts for arrows, Tord dared talk to him.

'You are from a good family, Berg,' Tord said. 'The richest people in the valley are your kin. Your kinsmen have served kings and fought in their bodyguard.'

'They have more often fought in the ranks of the rebels and done much damage to the kings,' Berg the Giant retorted.

'Your forefathers held grand feasts at Yule, as did you when you held your estates. There is room for hundreds of men and women on the benches of your great hall. It was built even before Saint Olaf brought baptism to the Oslo Fjord. You possessed ancient silver vessels and great drinking horns that were filled with mead and passed from man to man.'

Once again Berg the Giant had to look at the boy, who was now sitting up, his legs hanging over the side of the bed, his head resting in his hands and holding back the wild mop of hair that threatened to fall down over his eyes. His face had grown paler and more fine-featured from the ravages of his illness and fever still shone in his eyes. He was smiling at the images he was conjuring up for himself, at the decorated hall, at the silver vessels, at the guests in their festive clothes, at Berg the Giant sitting in the high seat in the hall of his forefathers. The farmer thought that, even in his feast day dress, no one had ever looked at him with eyes so bright with admiration or found him so magnificent as this boy found him in his torn garb of hides.

He was both moved and annoyed. This petty thief had no right to admire him. 'Were no feasts held in your home?' Berg asked.

Tord laughed. 'Out there in the skerries with Father and Mother? Father a wrecker and Mother a witch! No one wanted to come to our house.'

'Is your mother a witch?'

'Yes,' answered Tord, quite unconcerned. 'When the weather is stormy, she rides out to the ships the breakers are crashing over and claims all those who are cast into the sea.'

'What does she need them for?' Berg asked.

'Oh, a witch always needs corpses. She probably boils them to make ointments, or perhaps she eats them. On moonlit nights she sits out in the surf where it's at its whitest and the spray splashes over her. They say that she is searching for the fingers and eyes of shipwrecked children.'

'That's vile,' Berg said.

The boy answered with infinite confidence: 'It would be vile for other people but not for witches. They have to do it.'

Berg recognized that he was being confronted with a new way of looking at the world and its affairs. 'Do thieves have to steal just as witches have to cast spells?' he asked sharply.

'Certainly,' the boy answered. 'Everyone has to do what they are destined to do.' But then he added with a shy smile: 'There are some thieves who have never stolen.'

'Tell me what you mean!' Berg said.

The boy continued with his mysterious smile, proud of being an insoluble riddle. 'Talking about thieves who don't steal is the same as talking about birds that don't fly.'

Berg the Giant acted simple in order to learn more. 'No one can be called a thief without having stolen,' he said.

'Maybe not,' the boy said, pinching his lips as if to hold the words back. 'But what if someone had a father who stole?' he suggested after a while.

'People inherit estates and property,' the Giant replied, 'but no one is called a thief unless he earns the name for himself.'

Tord laughed quietly. 'But what if someone has a mother who begs and pleads with him to take the blame for his father's crime? And what if someone cheats the executioner and flees to the forest? And what if someone is sentenced to be an outlaw for the sake of a fishing net he has never seen?'

Berg the Giant smashed his fist down on the stone table. He was enraged. Here was this fine boy who had thrown away the whole of his life. He had no hope now of winning love or possessions or the respect of his fellows. The only things left for him were the misery and worry about getting food and clothing. And this fool had allowed him, Berg the Giant, to scorn him even though he was innocent. He scolded him in the harshest terms, but Tord was no more afraid of him than a sick child fears its mother's scolding for catching a cold by wading in a burn in springtime.

*

On one of these wide wooded hills lay a dark tarn. It was square, with shores so straight and corners so sharp that it looked as if it had been dug by man. On three sides it was surrounded by steep walls of rock to which spruce trees clung with roots as thick as an arm. Down by the tarn, where the covering of turf had been worn away over time, crooked and naked roots protruded from the water, twisting strangely round each other. They formed an endless mass of snakes, all trying to crawl up and out of the tarn at one and the same time and so becoming tangled and trapped. Or they were the heaped and blackened skeletons of drowned giants that the tarn was trying to cast ashore. Arms and legs twined around each other, long fingers dug down into the rock itself for support, mighty rib-cages formed arches that then supported ancient trees. In one case, however, the iron-hard arms and fingers of steel with which the spruce trees clung on had given way and the mighty north wind had hurled a tree in a wide arc out into the tarn from the rocks above. It landed crown first and stuck fast, deep in the mud at the bottom of the tarn, where its branches now gave a safe place of refuge for the fingerlings, while its roots stuck up from the water resembling a monster with many arms. It was these blackened and forked roots that helped give the tarn an atmosphere that was both frightening and evil.

On the fourth side of the tarn the hillside fell away and there a small foaming burn carried its water away. In order to find its only possible outfall, the burn was forced to seek a way between rocks and outcrops, thus creating a miniature world of islets, some of them no bigger than a tussock, others large enough to support a score or more trees.

Since the surrounding hills did not cut out all the sun, even broad-leaved trees were thriving here. Thirsty, grey-green alders and glabrous willows grew – as did birches, just as they always do when coniferous woods need to be held at bay. And there were bird-cherry and rowan – the trees that so often fringe forest meadows, filling them with scent and crowning them with beauty.

There, close to the outfall, grew a forest of reeds as tall as a man, making the sunlight fall upon the water with a greenish hue, just as it does on moss in a real forest. Among the reeds were open places – small, round pools on which water lilies floated. The tall reeds looked down gently and solemnly on these delicate beauties, which protected their white petals and yellow stamens within a leathery covering the moment the sun refused to show itself.

One sunny day the outlaws came to this tarn to fish. They waded out to two large rocks in the reed-bed and sat there casting bait for the big, green-streaked pike that lay sleeping close to the water's edge.

Without knowing it themselves these men, in their endless comings and goings in forests and mountains, had fallen as much under the power of natural forces as plants and animals. Sunshine made them open and courageous, but once the sun disappeared in the evening, they fell silent; and night, which seemed to them so much greater and mightier than day, made them timid and weak. And now, the green light that fell between the reeds and shaded the water dark green and golden bronze, bewitched them. All outward views were closed off. From time to time the reeds swayed in an imperceptible breeze, their stems rustling and the long ribbons of their leaves fluttering against the men's faces. Clad in grey animal hides, they sat there on the grey rocks, the colour of their furs mimicking the changes in the weathered, lichen-covered stones. Motionless and silent, each seemed to the other like a statue in stone, while the great fish with their rainbow-coloured backs swam among the reeds. While the men cast their hooks and watched the rings on the water spread through the reeds, the ripples seemed to grow ever stronger until at last they saw that their casts were not the only cause. A kelpie, half human and half glistening fish, lay sleeping in the edge of the water. She was lying on her back, her whole body under the water and so well hidden that they hadn't noticed her before. It was her breathing that prevented the ripples from coming to rest. But there was nothing strange about her lying there, and when, just a moment later, she was gone, they could not be sure she'd been more than an optical illusion.

The green light seeped through their eyes into their brains like a mild drug. Sunk in listless thought, the men sat and stared, seeing sights among the reeds that they did not dare confide to each other. The catch was poor. The day was devoted to dreams and revelations.

Then the sound of oars came from among the reeds and, as if waking from slumber, they started. A moment later a boat came into view. It was heavy, no more than a roughly hollowed tree-trunk, its cracks full of moss and the oars thin as sticks. It was being rowed by a young girl who was picking water lilies. She had big dark eyes and dark-brown hair gathered in heavy plaits, and she was strangely pale. But the pallor was tinged with pink rather than grey. Her cheeks were no more highly coloured than the rest of her face, her lips scarcely so. She wore a white linen smock, a leather belt with a gold buckle and her kirtle was blue with red edging. She rowed past close to the outlaws without seeing them. They remained motionless, holding their breath, not from fear of being seen but simply to be able to watch her closely. As soon as she was gone, it was as if they changed from statues into men. They looked at one another and smiled.

'She was as white as the lilies,' one of them said.

'Her eyes were as dark as the water below the roots of the trees.'

Their spirits were so lifted that they felt an urge to laugh, to really laugh as no one by this tarn had ever laughed before, to laugh so that the rocky walls thundered and echoed, so that the roots of the spruces were shaken loose with fright.

'Did you find her beautiful?' Berg the Giant asked.

'Oh, I don't know. I saw her for such a short time. Perhaps she was.'

'You didn't dare look at her. You probably thought she was a mermaid.'

And once again they shook with the same incongruous merriment.

*

Once, when he was a child, Tord had seen a drowned man. He'd found the corpse on the shore in broad daylight and not been in the least afraid, but at night he'd had dreadful dreams. He saw a sea in which every wave rolled a dead man towards his feet. He saw, too, how all the rocks and islands in the skerries were covered in drowned men who were dead and belonged to the sea, but who could still speak and move and threaten him with their shrivelled white hands.

This happened to him again now. The girl seen among the reeds returned in his dreams. He met her on the bottom of the tarn where the sunlight fell with a light much greener than among the reeds, and now he had time to see that she was beautiful. He dreamed he'd crawled up on to the roots of the huge spruce in the middle of the dark tarn but the tree rocked and swayed so much that at times he went right under the water. Sometimes she appeared on the small islands. She stood beneath the red rowans and laughed at him. In his last dream he took things to the point of her kissing him. By then it was morning and he heard that Berg the Giant was up and about but he stubbornly kept his eyes shut in order to continue dreaming. When he woke he was dizzy and stunned by what had happened to him during the night. He thought about the girl much more than he'd done the day before.

Towards evening it occurred to him to ask Berg the Giant whether he knew her name.

Berg looked at him as if testing him. 'I suppose it's as well you be told straight away,' he said. 'She is Unn. She is a kinswoman of mine.'

Tord knew then that it was for the sake of this pale maid that Berg the Giant was an outlaw condemned to forest and mountain. Tord tried to recall what he knew about her.

Unn was the daughter of a big landowner. Her mother was dead so she ruled in her father's house. This pleased her, for she loved power and had no desire to take a husband.

Unn and Berg the Giant were cousins and it had long been said that Berg preferred to sit and jest with Unn and her maidservants than to work on his own estates. When the great Yule feast was held at Berg's house his wife had invited a monk from Dragsmark* because she wanted him to reproach Berg for favouring another woman and forgetting her. Because of his appearance – he was very fat and pure white – this monk was abhorrent to Berg and to many other people. The tonsure around his bald head, the eyebrows above his watery eyes, the colour of his face, his hands and the habit he wore, all these were white. There were many who found the sight of him hard to bear.

Within the hearing of all the guests at the festive table the monk spoke, for he was fearless and thought his words would have more effect if they were heard by many: 'It is often said that the cuckoo is the worst of birds because it doesn't rear its young in its own nest. There is a man sitting among us who does not attend to his own home and children but seeks his pleasures with another woman. I will call him the worst of men.'

Unn rose to her feet. 'Berg,' she said, 'these words are spoken to you and to me. I have never suffered such an insult. But then, my father is not present at this feast.' She wanted to leave but Berg had run after her. 'Stay there!' she said. 'I never wish see you again.'

He caught her up at the entrance and asked her what he could do to make her stay. With fire in her eyes she answered that he should know that for himself. Then Berg went and killed the monk.

Berg and Tord were now following the same train of thought and after a while Berg said: 'You should have seen Unn when the white monk was slain. My wife gathered our small children around her and cursed her: she turned the children's faces towards Unn so they would remember forever the woman who had made their father a murderer. But Unn stood there so calm and beautiful that men trembled. She thanked me for the deed and bade me flee to the forest at once. She exhorted me not to become a robber and not to wield the knife again unless I did so for a cause as just as this one.'

'Your exploit had exalted her,' Tord said.

Berg the Giant now found himself facing the same thing in the boy as he had wondered at before. He was like a heathen, worse than a heathen, he never condemned what was unjust. He felt no responsibility. What must happen must happen. He knew of God and Christ and the saints, but only by name, just as one knows the gods of foreign lands. The ghosts of the skerries were his gods. His mother and her sorcery had taught him to believe in the spirits of the dead.

It was then that Berg the Giant undertook a task that was as foolish as tying a rope for his own neck. He opened the ignorant boy's eyes to the greatness of God, the Lord of Righteousness, the avenger of evil deeds, who casts wrongdoers down into the abyss of eternal pain. And he taught him to love Christ and His mother and the holy men and women who lay before the throne of God with their hands raised to shield the hosts of sinners from the wrath of the great avenger. He taught him everything that man does to propitiate the wrath of God. He showed him the hosts of pilgrims making their way to the holy places, the penitents who inflict suffering upon themselves, and the monks who flee the worldly life.

As Berg spoke the boy became ever more eager and ever paler. His eyes grew wide as though he were seeing horrific visions. Berg the Giant wanted to stop but the flow of his thoughts gripped him and he continued to speak. Night sank down over them, the dark forest night in which wolves howl. God was so close to them that they saw His throne obscure the stars and His avenging angels descending to the treetops. But below them the flames of the underworld flared up even to the surface of the earth and licked voraciously at this trembling refuge of anguished mankind.

*

Autumn came and brought hard storms. Tord went alone out into the forest to check their traps and tackle. Berg the Giant sat at home mending his clothes. Tord's route took him up a tree-clad hill. There was a broad path.

Every gust of the storm capable of penetrating the tight tangle of trees drove rustling whorls of dry leaves along the path. Time after time Tord thought that someone was walking behind him and he often looked back. Sometimes he stopped to listen, but then realised it was only the leaves and the wind and so he continued on his way. No sooner did he start walking again than he heard someone dancing on silken feet up the slope. The tripping of children's little feet. Elves and sprites were at play behind him. When he turned round there was no one there. Still no one. He clenched his fists at the rustling leaves and walked on.

That did not silence them and they began making other sounds instead. Behind him there were hissing and panting sounds. A huge viper came slithering along, its tongue hanging from its mouth and dripping venom while its glistening body glinted against the withered leaves. A wolf padded along beside the snake, a great lean grey-wolf ready to fasten its jaws on his neck when the viper coiled between his feet and bit his heel. Sometimes they both kept silent as if to approach him unnoticed, but immediately afterwards they would betray themselves by hissing and panting, and sometimes the wolf's claws would clatter noisily on a stone. Against his will Tord began to walk faster and faster but the animals came swiftly after him. When he believed they were only two steps behind and ready to pounce, he turned round. There was nothing there, as he had known the whole time.

He sat down on a stone to rest. The dry leaves played around his feet as if to divert him. All the leaves of the forest were there: the small, bright yellow leaves of the birch, rowan leaves with their many shades of red, the dry brownish-black leaves of the elm, the tough bright-red leaves of the aspen and the yellowish green of the willow. Now they were shrivelled and decayed, scarred and ragged, so different from the soft, bright-green and delicate surfaces that had opened from the buds a few months before.

'Sinners!' the boy said. 'Sinners! There is nothing that is pure in the sight of God. The flames of His wrath have already reached you.'

When he set off on his way again he saw the forest below him moving like a storm-driven sea, but down on the path everything was calm and still. And now he heard what he had not heard before. The forest was full of voices.

There were whispers like mournful songs, like coarse threats and thundering oaths. There was laughter and wailing like the din made by crowds of people. His thoughts were driven wild by all this, egged on and incited by the rustling and hissing that seemed both to be something and yet nothing. He felt again the fear of death as he had felt it when lying on the floor of the cave while the hunt for them passed through the forest. He heard branches breaking, the heavy tramp of the hunters, the ring of their weapons, thunderous shouts and the wild and bloodthirsty murmurings of the host.

But this was not all that was present in the storm in the forest. There was something else, something even more terrifying, voices that he could not interpret, a hubbub of sounds that seemed to be speaking to him in a strange tongue. He had heard mightier storms than this tearing through the rigging, but never before had he heard the wind play on a harp with so many strings. Every tree had its own voice and the sound of the spruce was not that of the aspen, nor the poplar that of the rowan. Every ravine had its own note, the resounding echo of every cliff its own tone. And in the monstrous orchestra of this forest storm, the roar of the burns and the barking of the fox could also be heard. All of this he could interpret, but there were other, stranger sounds. It was these that were causing the screams and sneers and lamentation within him to grow until they contended with the storm itself.

He liked the open sea and the bare skerries. He had always been afraid when alone in the gloom of the forest where spirits and shades lurked among the trees.

Now, all at once, he heard who was speaking in the storm. It was God, the great avenger, the God of Righteousness was hunting him because of his friend. He was demanding he should deliver up the monk's murderer for vengeance.

Tord began to speak in the midst of the storm. He told God what he'd wanted to do but lacked the strength. He'd wanted to speak to Berg the Giant and beg him to make his peace with God, but he'd been too timid. Timidity had made him silent. 'When I learned that the earth is ruled by a righteous God,' the boy called out, 'I understood that he was lost. I have lain and wept for my friend through many long nights. I knew that God would find him wherever he hid. But I did not have the strength to speak, to teach him to understand. I was struck dumb because my love for him was so great. Do not demand that I speak to him! Do not demand that the seas should rise up to the heights of the mountains!'

The boy fell silent, as did the deep voice in the storm that had been the voice of God to him. All at once the wind dropped, a bright sun shone and sounds like the splash of oars and the quiet rustle of stiff reeds were heard. These gentle sounds brought the image of Unn to the boy's mind. An outlaw can achieve nothing, not estates nor women nor esteem among men but if he were to betray Berg, he would be admitted to the protection of the law. But Unn must love Berg after what he had done for her. There was no way out of all this.

As the storm rose once more, every so often he heard footsteps and breathless panting behind him again. He dared not look back for now he knew that the white monk was there. He was coming from the feast at Berg the Giant's home, spattered with blood and with a gaping axe-wound in his forehead. And he was whispering: 'Betray him, inform on him, save his soul! Deliver his body to the flames so that his soul may be spared! Deliver him up to the long torment of the rack so that his soul may have time to repent!'

Tord ran. All of these horrors, which in themselves were nothing, grew into a great fear that wormed its way incessantly into his soul. He wanted to get away from it all. When he began to run, the deep and awesome voice that was the voice of God began again to roar. God himself was harrying him with terrors to make him deliver up the murderer. To the boy, the crime of Berg the Giant appeared more loathsome than ever. An unarmed man had been murdered, a man of God pierced with shining steel. That was in defiance of the Lord of all the worlds. And the murderer dared live! He dared rejoice in the shining of the sun and the fruits of the earth as if the arm of the Almighty was too short to reach him.

The boy stopped, clenched his fists and howled a threat. Then, like a madman, he ran from the forest, ran from the realm of terrors, ran down to the valley.

*

Tord needed do no more than state his business and ten farmers were immediately ready to accompany him. They decided that

Tord should go up to the cave alone so as not to arouse Berg's suspicions. And as he went, he was to scatter peas so that the farmers could find their way.

When Tord entered the cave the outlaw was asleep, sitting up on the stone bench. The light from the fire was poor and his work seemed to have gone badly. The boy's heart filled with compassion. Berg the Giant, that fine figure of a man, now seemed so impoverished and unfortunate. And his life, the only thing he owned, was to be taken from him. Tord began to weep. 'What's the matter?' Berg asked. 'Are you ill? Has something frightened you?'

Then, for the first time, Tord spoke about his fear. 'It was horrible in the forest. I heard phantoms and I saw ghosts. I saw white monks.'

'By the blood of Christ, boy!'

'They chanted masses at me the whole way up Bredfjäll. I ran, but they stayed with me and sang. How can I ever be rid of their din? What have they got to do with me? I think they should be saying mass for someone more in need of it than me.'

'Have you gone mad tonight, Tord?'

Tord spoke, hardly knowing the words he used. All his shyness left him and the words flowed from his lips unhindered. 'They are all white monks, white, deathly pale. All of them have blood on their cowls. They pull their hoods down over their brows but even so the wound still shows up clearly. The great red gaping wound from the blow of the axe.'

'The great red gaping wound from the blow of the axe?'

'Am I the one supposed to have struck the blow? Why should I be the one to see it?'

Berg the Giant, pale and with a terrible earnestness, said: 'Tord, Heaven alone knows what it means or why you see axe wounds, for I killed the monk with two thrusts of my knife.'

Tord was now standing in front of Berg, twisting his hands together and trembling. 'They are demanding that I hand you in. They want to force me to betray you.'

'Who? The monks?'

'Yes, of course, the monks. They show me visions. They show me the girl Unn. They show me the shining sunlit sea. They show me the dwellings of the fish and there is dancing and merrymaking there. I shut my eyes but I can still see it. Leave me in peace, I say to them. My friend has committed murder but he is not an evil man. Leave me be and I shall speak to him so that he repents and does penance. He will acknowledge his sin and journey to the grave of Christ. We shall travel together to places so holy that all sin is cleansed from those who visit them.'

'What is the monks' answer?' Berg asked. 'They do not want me saved. They want to see me on the rack and at the stake.'

'Am I to betray my dearest friend, I ask them,' Tord continued. 'He is everything I have in this world. He has saved me from the bear that had claws at my throat. Together we have frozen and suffered all kinds of troubles. He spread his own bear-skin over me when I lay ill. I have carried wood and water for him, I have guarded him as he slept and I have frustrated his enemies. Why do they believe that I am the sort of man to betray a friend? My friend will soon go to the priest and make his confession and then we shall go together to the land of reconciliation.'

Berg listened earnestly, his eyes keenly watching Tord's face. 'You must go to the priest yourself and tell him the truth,' he said. 'You must go out among the people again.'

'But how will it help me if I go alone? It is because of your sin that the dead monk and all the shades are pursuing me. Can you not see how you fill me with horror? You have raised your hand against God himself. No crime is like your crime. I would be pleased to see you broken on the wheel, for fortunate is the man who takes his punishment in this world and escapes the wrath to come. Why did you tell me about the righteousness. of God? It is you who is forcing me to betray you. Spare me from this sin! Go to the priest.' And the boy fell on his knees before Berg.

The murderer laid his hand on the boy's head and looked at him. He began to measure his sin by the yardstick of his companion's anguish and his soul began to recognize its enormity and horror. He saw that he was in conflict with the will that rules the world. Remorse entered his heart.

'Alas that I did what I did!' he said. 'What lies before me is too heavy to be met willingly. If I hand myself to the priests they will torture me with hours of torment. They will roast me on slow fires. Does not this life of misery that we lead here in fear and need make sufficient recompense? Have I not lost my home and my estates? Am I not living apart from my friends and all that gives a man joy? What more can be demanded?'

When he spoke like this, Tord leapt up horror-struck. 'Can you repent?' he shouted. 'Can my words move your heart? How was I to know that? Come at once! Come and flee! There is still time.'

Then Berg leapt to his feet, too: 'You have already done it then!'

'Yes, yes! I have betrayed you. Come quickly! Come on now, since you can repent. They will let us go. We shall escape them.'

The murderer bent down to the floor where his ancestral battle-axe lay. 'You son of a thief!' he said spitting out the words. 'I believed you and loved you!'

But when Tord saw him bend down for the axe he knew that his life was at stake. He snatched his own axe from his belt and struck at Berg before the Giant could straighten up. The blade sliced and whistled through the air and sank into Berg's bowed head. Berg the Giant fell headfirst to the ground and his body followed. Blood and brains spurted out and the axe fell from the wound. In the matted hair on Berg's head Tord saw the great, red, gaping hole made by the blow from the axe.

Now the farmers came rushing in. They rejoiced and praised Tord's deed. 'This will stand your case in good stead,' they said to him.

Tord looked down at his hands as if he could see there the fetters by which he had been dragged to kill the man he loved. Like those of the Fenris Wolf,* they were forged of nothing: they were made of the green light of the reed-bed, the play of shadows in the forest, the song of the storm, the rustling of the leaves, the enchantment of dreams. And he said aloud: 'God is great.'

But his thoughts returned to their former course. He fell to his knees by the corpse and put his arm under its head.

'Don't do anything to him!' he said. 'He repents. He wants to make a pilgrimage to the holy tombs. He isn't dead but do not chain him! We were ready to go when he fell. The white monk did not want him to repent but God, the God of Righteousness, loves repentance.'

He lay there beside the corpse, talking to it, weeping and begging the dead man to wake. The farmers prepared a bier of spears. They wanted to bear the corpse of the farmer down to his farm. They respected the dead man and spoke quietly in his presence. When they lifted him onto the bier, Tord stood up, shook the hair from his face and spoke in a voice that trembled with sobs: 'Tell Unn, who made Berg the Giant a murderer, that he was killed by Tord the fisherman, whose father is a wrecker and whose mother is a witch, because Berg taught him that righteousness is the foundation of this world.'

(From *Osynliga länkar,* 1894.)

Notes

110 *his tongue tasted as if he had eaten unholy horse flesh*: the eating of horse flesh was associated with pagan practices and thus discouraged when the Nordic countries converted to Christianity.

116 *Dragsmark*: the monastery at Dragsmark in Bohuslän, then a part of Norway, was founded before 1260 and secularised at the Reformation in 1519. Only a few ruins are still visible. The monastery was occupied by the Premonstratensian Order, known as the White Canons from the colour of their habit. Formally speaking they were canons regular, not monks, which meant that their work was to go out and preach and provide pastoral care in surrounding parishes.

124 *Fenris Wolf*: the monstrous wolf of Norse mythology, the offspring of the trickster-god Loki. The gods, fearing the wolf's strength, bound him with magical bonds that consisted of a cat's footsteps, the beard of a woman, the breath of a fish and much more. At Ragnarök (Doomsday), the wolf will break free and devour the sun and the god Odin.

THE SILVER MINE

Silvergruvan

Translated by Peter Graves

King Gustav III* was travelling through Dalarna. He was in a great hurry, wanting to make the whole journey at a wild pace. Galloping at such speed, the horses looked like leather thongs stretched out along the road and the carriage was taking the corners on two wheels. For all that, the king still had his head out of the carriage window shouting at the coachman: 'Why can't you get a move on? Do you think you are driving over eggshells?'

Given that they were driving at such a mad pace on poor country roads, it would have been a miracle if the reins, harnesses and carriages had held up. And they didn't: at the foot of a steep hill the shaft snapped and the king was left sitting there. The courtiers leapt out of the carriage and berated the coachman, which did little to mend the damage. There was no hope of continuing the journey until the carriage was repaired.

When the courtiers looked around to see what they could find for the king's entertainment while he was waiting, they noticed a church tower rising above a cluster of trees a short distance farther along the road. They suggested to the king that he drive on to the church in one of the coaches used by his attendants. It was Sunday, after all, and the king would be able to pass the time by attending the church service while waiting for his great royal coach to be mended.

The king agreed to the suggestion and drove on to the

church. The earlier part of his journey had involved many hours driving through dark forests, whereas everything here looked more cheerful: quite big fields and villages and the Dala River gliding along bright and splendid between great clumps of alder bushes.

But the king's bad luck continued in that the organist was already playing the recessional hymn and the congregation had started to come out just as the king was stepping down from the coach outside the church. As the people were walking past, the king stood motionless on the spot, one foot still in the coach and the other on the step, and just watched them. They were the finest looking people he'd ever seen. All the men were above average height and had sensible, earnest faces, and the women were fine and proper in all their sabbath dignity.

The king had spent the whole of the previous day talking about the desolation of the country he was passing through and time after time he'd said to his courtiers: 'Surely this must be the very poorest part of my realm that I'm seeing here'.

Now, however, observing the people dressed up in their fine local dress, he forgot all about the poverty. His heart warmed and he said to himself: 'The King of Sweden is not as badly off as his enemies think. As long as my subjects look like this, I'll certainly be in a position to defend both my faith and my country.'

He commanded his courtiers to announce to the people that the stranger standing among them was their king and they should gather round for him to speak to them.

And so, from the high steps outside the vestry, the king made a speech to his people. The narrow step on which he stood is there to this very day.

The king began by giving them an account of the perilous state in which the kingdom found itself.* He said the Swedes had been attacked both by Russians and by Danes and, whereas this wouldn't have posed great difficulties in other circumstances, the army was currently so full of traitors that he dared not rely on it. Which is why he'd had no other choice but to set off round the country himself to ask his subjects whether they wanted to join the traitors or whether they would be loyal to their king and help with men and money so he could save their fatherland.

The country folk listened in silence while the king was speaking and when he'd finished they showed no sign of approval or disapproval.

The king himself thought he'd been very eloquent. Tears had come into his eyes several times while he was speaking. But since the people remained standing there looking anxious, uncertain and unable to bring themselves to answer him, his brow furrowed and he looked displeased.

The country people could see that the king was starting to find the delay tedious and finally one of them stepped forward.

'Now, you must be aware, King Gustav, that we weren't expecting a royal visit to our parish today,' the farmer said, 'and that's why we aren't ready to give you an answer promptly. I suggest you go into the vestry and speak to our minister, while we discuss among ourselves everything you've told us.'

The king recognised he wasn't going to get a better answer than that immediately and thought the sensible thing would be to follow the farmer's advice.

When he entered the vestry there was no one there apart from a man who looked like an old farmer. He was tall and stocky, with big hands marked by heavy work. The man was dressed in leather breeches and a long, white homespun coat just like all the other men and there was no sign of a collar or a cassock.

The man stood up and bowed when the king entered.

'I thought I'd find the minister in here,' the king said.

The man's face flushed a little. Seeing that the king took him to be a farmer, he was too mortified to admit that he actually was the minister of the parish.

'Well, the minister is usually here at this time,' he said.

The king sat down on a big, high-armed chair that used to be in the vestry in those days. It's still there today, in fact, more or less unchanged apart from the gilded royal crown the congregation has since attached to the back of it.

'Do you have a good minister in this parish?' the king asked, wanting to show an interest in the situation of the farmers.

When the king questioned him in this way, the minister thought there was no way he could admit who he actually was. 'Better for the king to carry on believing I'm just a farmer', he thought, and so he responded that the minister was good enough, that he preached the word of God in a pure and clear manner and that he tried to live as he taught.

The king thought this was high praise but, having a keen ear, he noticed just a touch of hesitance in the tone.

'All the same, it does sound rather as if you're not entirely satisfied with the minister,' he said.

'Well, he is a bit self-willed,' the man said, wanting to voice some mild criticism. His idea was that should the king later discover who he was, he wouldn't think the minister had been blowing his own trumpet. 'There are certainly some people who say that the minister wants to be the only one to have a say in the parish,' he continued.

'He does seem to have managed and done everything in the best possible way,' the king said. He didn't like the farmer complaining about a man set over him. 'It looks to me as if good practice and traditional simplicity are the order of the day here.'

'The people are fine enough, I suppose,' the minister said, 'but they live their lives in poverty and isolation. They would probably be no better than any other folk if the temptations of this world were closer at hand.'

'I imagine there's little risk of that happening,' the king said, shrugging his shoulders.

He said nothing more and started drumming his fingers on the table. He thought his gracious exchange with this farmer had lasted quite long enough and he was wondering when the others would be ready to respond to him.

'These country folk aren't exactly eager to help their king out,' he thought. 'If I had my coach, I'd be on my way and leave them to their deliberations.'

For his part, the minister was troubled. He was in two minds as to how to resolve an important issue he needed to decide. He was glad he hadn't told the king who he was and now he felt he could talk to the king about the sort of thing he wouldn't have been able to mention otherwise.

So, after a little while, the minister broke his silence and asked the king whether it was really the case that their enemies were threatening and the realm was in danger.

The king, however, thought this fellow ought to have enough sense not to bother him further. He just gave him a hard look and did not answer.

'I am asking this because, since I was in here, I was unable to hear properly,' the minister said. 'But if that really is the situation, I can tell you that the minister of this parish may be able to furnish the king with as much money as he needs.'

'I thought you said a little while ago that everyone around here was poor,' the king said, thinking the fellow had no idea what he was talking about.

'Yes, that is true,' the minister replied, 'and the minister doesn't own any more than anyone else. But if Your Majesty would be gracious enough to listen for a moment, I will tell you how and why the minister has the power to help you.'

'You have my leave to speak,' the king said. 'You appear to find it easier to get the words out than your friends and neighbours out there, who seem incapable of deciding what it is they have to say to me.'

'It's not exactly easy to respond to a king. In the end, I fear it will be up to the minister to do so on behalf of everyone else.'

The king crossed his legs, settled deep into the armchair, folded his arms and let his head fall on his chest.

'Right, you can start now,' the king said, his voice sounding as if he was already asleep.

'Once upon a time five men from this parish went out into the forest to hunt elk,' the minister began. 'One of them was the minister we are talking about. Two of the others were soldiers called Olof and Erik Svärd, the fourth man was the innkeeper in this village, and the fifth was a farmer by the name of Israels Per Persson.'

'No need to bother me with so many names,' the king muttered, letting his head fall to one side.

'These men were good hunters,' the minister went on, 'and luck was usually on their side, but that day they walked for miles and hours without any success. Eventually, they gave up the hunt and sat down on the ground to talk. They talked about there not being a single spot fit for cultivation in the whole forest: there was nothing but mountain and bog. "Our Lord didn't do right by us when he gave us such poor country to live in," one of them said. "Elsewhere there are places people can acquire riches in abundance, whereas here, however much we toil and slave, we can scarcely win our daily bread."'

The minister paused for a moment as if uncertain whether the king had heard him, but the king moved his little finger to show he was still awake.

'Just then, while the hunters were talking like this, the minister caught sight of something glistening in the bedrock, just where his foot had kicked away the moss. "It's a remarkable mountain, this," he thought and then proceeded to kick away another lump of moss. He picked up a splinter of the stone that had come loose with the moss and it shone in the same way as all the rest. "This can't actually be lead, can it?" he said, at which the others rushed over and used the butts of their guns to clear away more moss. Once they had done so, they could see quite clearly that there was a wide vein of ore running through the rock. "What do you think this might be?" the minister asked. The men chipped off some splinters of the rock and bit them – "It must be lead or zinc, anyway," they said. "And the whole mountain is made of it," the innkeeper added.'

When the minister reached this point in his story, the king's head was seen to lift just a little and one eye opened. 'Do you know whether any of them knew anything at all about ores and rock types?' he asked. 'No, they didn't,' the minister replied, at which the king's head sank back again and both eyes closed.

'The minister and the other hunters were overjoyed,' the speaker continued, undeterred by the king's indifference. 'They thought they'd discovered something that was going to make them rich – and maybe their descendants, too. "I shall never have to work again – I'll be rich enough to do nothing all week and to drive to church on Sundays in a golden carriage!" one of them said.

'Generally speaking, these men were sensible fellows, but this great discovery went to their heads and made them talk like children. But they still had enough sense to replace the moss and hide the vein of ore. And they made a careful note of the position before setting off home.

'When they parted, they agreed that the minister should go to Falun* and ask the inspector of mines what sort of ore this was. He should return as quickly as possible and, in the meantime the others swore solemn oaths not to reveal the location of the ore to a single soul.'

The king raised his head a little but didn't say a word to interrupt the speaker. He seemed to be beginning to believe that the latter really did have something worthwhile to tell him and was not about to allow the king's indifference put him off.

'So the minister set off with several samples of ore in his pocket. He was as pleased as the rest of them at the idea of becoming rich. He thought he'd rebuild the manse, which at present was no better than a peasant's cottage, and he'd marry a dean's daughter he was fond of. Until now he'd been expecting to wait many years for her: being poor and humble, he knew it would be a long time before he was in a position to marry.

'The minister's journey to Falun took two days and, once there, he had a day to wait since the inspector of mines was away. Finally, he was able to meet him and show him the samples of ore. The inspector took them in his hand, looked first at them and then at the minister. The minister told him he'd found them on a hill back in his home parish and was wondering whether it might possibly be lead. "No, it's not lead," the inspector said. "Could it possibly be zinc, then?" the minister asked. "No, it's not zinc either," the inspector said.

'The minister felt all his hopes sinking. He hadn't been so depressed for many a day. "Do you have many rocks of this type in your parish?" the inspector of mines asked. "We have a whole mountain of it," the minister said. Then the inspector went up to the minister, patted him on the shoulder and said: "See to it that you use your find in such a way that it profits both you and the kingdom – for this is silver!" "Really?" the minister said hesitantly and uncertainly. "I see, so it's silver then."

'The inspector of mines now began telling him how to go about acquiring legal rights to the mine and giving him many bits of good advice, but the minister's head was in a daze and he didn't hear what was being said to him. All he could think about was how wonderful it was to have a whole mountain of silver ore lying waiting back at home in his poor parish.'

The king raised his head so suddenly that the minister cut short his account.

'And I suppose,' the king said, 'that when you got home and started work on the mine, you quickly realised that the inspector of mines had merely been making a fool of you?'

'Oh no,' the minister said, 'the inspector hadn't been making a fool of me.'

'You may continue,' the king said, settling back to listen.

'When the minister eventually returned home and was driving through his parish,' the minister went on, 'he thought that his first duty was to inform his fellow hunters about the value of their discovery. Since he was passing the innkeeper Sten Stensson's place, he decided to go in and tell him that what they'd found was silver. When he stopped outside the gate, however, he saw there were sheets hanging over the windows and a broad pathway of chopped spruce leading up to the front steps. "Who is it who has died?" the minister asked a boy who was leaning on the fence. "The innkeeper himself," the boy answered, before proceeding to inform the minister that the innkeeper had drunk himself senseless every single day for the last week. "He downed so much schnapps – oh, what a quantity of schnapps he put away!" the boy said. "How can that be possible?" the minister asked. "The innkeeper never used to drink enough to get drunk." "Well, it's like this," the boy said, "he drank because he said he'd found a mine. He said he was so rich he'd never need to do anything but drink. And yesterday evening, drunk as he was, he went out driving, overturned his cart and was killed."

'After hearing this, the minister drove on homeward, saddened by what he'd heard. He'd been so happy before, so full of joy at having such great news to impart.

'He had gone no more than a short distance, when he saw Israels Per Persson walking along. He looked to be his usual self and the minister thought it augured well that good fortune hadn't gone to his head, too. He would now make him happy by telling him he was a rich man. "Good day!" Per Persson greeted him. "Are you on your way back from Falun now?" "I am indeed," the minister said, "and I can tell you that things went better than we imagined. The inspector of mines said that what we'd found was silver ore."

'The moment he heard this, Per Persson looked as if the earth had opened under him. "What? What are you saying? Is it silver?" "Yes," the minister answered, "we're going to be rich men now, all of us, and we'll be able to live like lords." "No, really? Really silver?" Per Persson repeated, looking more and more downcast. "Yes, definitely silver," the minister said. "You mustn't think I'm trying to deceive you. You mustn't be afraid to be happy." "Happy?" said Per Persson. "How can I possibly be happy? I thought that what we'd found was nothing but fool's gold. So, I thought, better safe than sorry and I sold my share of the mine to Olof Svärd for a hundred daler."

'Filled with despair, he stood and wept on the high road as the minister drove on.

'On arriving back at home, the minister sent a servant to inform Olof Svärd and his brother that what they'd found was silver. He'd had quite enough of taking the good news around himself.

'But sitting alone that evening, the minister couldn't help but rejoice in his good fortune. He stepped out into the darkness and stood on the hillock where he was intending to build his new manse. It would be a grand building, of course, as splendid as a bishop's residence. He stayed outside for a long time that night, not confining himself just to the building of the new manse. There would be so much wealth in the parish, he thought, that people would flock there in such numbers that a whole city might grow up around the mine. And then he would have to build a new church to replace the old one – and that, no doubt, would require a good deal of his wealth. But even that wasn't enough for him: he imagined that when the church was ready, the king and many bishops would come to its consecration. The king would be pleased with the church, but he would remark that there was no accommodation for him –

the king – to lodge in. And then he'd be given leave to build a palace for the king in the new city.'

Just then one of the king's courtiers opened the vestry door and announced that the great royal coach had been mended.

The king's first thought was to depart immediately, but then, on reflection, he said to the minister: 'Tell me the whole story, now, right to the end, but do hurry it along. We know how the man dreamed and how he thought, but we want to know how he acted.'

'Well, while the minister was still completely lost in this dream world,' the minister continued, 'news reached him that Israels Per Persson had done away with himself. He'd been unable to bear the fact that he'd sold his share of the mine. No doubt he'd thought how impossible it would be to endure watching someone else enjoying daily the wealth that could have been his.'

The king sat up a little straighter in the chair and now he kept both eyes open. 'My goodness,' he said, 'if I were the minister, I do believe I'd have been sick and tired of that mine.'

'The king is a rich man, of course,' the minister said. 'Well, he has quite sufficient anyway, but it's very different for a poor minister who owns nothing. When the poor fellow saw that God's blessing was not favouring his enterprise, he thought instead, "I won't do any more dreaming about bringing honour and advantage to myself with all this wealth. But I can't just leave the silver in the ground, can I? I must extract it so as to provide for the poor and needy. I shall work the mine to help the whole parish onto its feet."

'Which is why the minister went to visit Olof Svärd one day to talk to him and his brother about what they should do about the silver mountain. As he was approaching the soldiers' croft,* he met a cart with an escort of armed farmers. In the cart sat a man with his hands tied behind his back and his ankles tied with rope.

'As the minister was passing the cart, it stopped for a moment and he had time to look at the prisoner. It wasn't easy to see who it was since the prisoner's head was covered, but the minister thought he could recognise Olof Svärd.

'He heard the prisoner ask the men guarding him to allow him a few words with the minister, and so the minister went closer and the prisoner turned to him: "You will soon be the only one who knows where that silver mountain is," Olof said. "What do you mean by that, Olof?" the minister asked. "Well, minister, the fact is that the moment we got to hear that it was a mountain of silver, my brother and I were unable to remain the good friends we'd been before and we took to quarrelling the whole time. Yesterday evening we started arguing about which of the five of us was the first to find the mine. We ended up fighting and I killed my brother, not before he'd given me this scar on my forehead to remember him by. I shall be hanged now and you'll be left as the only one who knows anything about the mine. Which is why I have one request to you." "Tell me!" the minister said, "and I'll do what I can for you." "You know that I'm leaving many small children behind," the soldier began, but the minister cut him off. "You can put your mind at rest about that. They'll get your share of the mine, exactly as if you had lived." "No," Olof Svärd said. "What I wanted to ask of you was something quite different. Don't allow any of them to have any part of what that mine may produce!"

'The minister recoiled a step and stood in silence, unable to find an answer. "Unless you promise me this, I can't go to my death in peace," the prisoner said. "Well," the minister said slowly and reluctantly, "I promise to do as you wish."

'With that, the murderer was driven away, leaving the minister standing there on the road wondering how to go about keeping the promise he had just given. All the way home he thought of the wealth he had been so happy about. But what if the people in this parish were simply unable to countenance riches? Four men, who had previously been proud and upright fellows, were already ruined. In his mind's eye, he saw the whole parish before him and he imagined how the silver mine would ruin them one by one. Was it right for him, responsible as he was for the care of these poor people's souls, to bring down upon them something that could lead to their downfall?'

All at once the king pulled himself up straight in the chair and stared at the speaker. 'I must say this!' he said, 'I really must! You are giving me to understand that the minister, even in a district as remote as this, is a man with a true and honest heart.'

'Then,' the minister continued, 'as if what had occurred so far wasn't enough, the moment news of the mine spread among the parishioners, they ceased working and lazed about waiting for the moment great riches came their way. And all the vagrants in the surrounding area poured in and the minister heard nothing but talk of drinking and brawling.

'Many people did nothing apart from scouring the forest in search of the mine. The minister noticed, too, that whenever he left home, people came creeping after him in an attempt to steal his secret should he be going to the silver mountain.

'When things had come to this pass, the minister summoned the farmers to a meeting.

'First of all, he reminded them of all the misfortunes the discovery of the silver mountain had brought down upon them, and he asked them whether they were going to let themselves be ruined or whether they were willing to save themselves. He told them they could not expect him, the man who was their minister, to contribute to their downfall. His decision was not to reveal the location of the silver mountain to anyone – and never to use it to enrich himself. He asked the farmers about their intentions for the future: if they were going to continue hunting for the mine in the hope of becoming rich, he would move so far away that not even the slightest rumour of their misery could reach him, but if they were willing to forget all thoughts of the mine and become as they had been before, he would stay among them. "But remember this," he said, "whatever you decide, no one will ever learn anything from me about the silver mountain!"'

'And?' the king said, 'Which did the farmers choose?'

'They did what their minister wanted,' the speaker said. 'They understood that he had their good in mind in that he was prepared to stay poor for their sakes. They sent him away into the forest to hide the vein of ore under brushwood and rocks so thoroughly that neither they nor their descendants would ever find it.'

'So the minister has lived here just as poor as the rest of them ever since, has he?'

'Yes,' the speaker answered, 'he has lived here as poor as the rest of them.'

'Surely he must have married and built a new manse for himself?' the king said.

'No, he's never been able to afford marriage and he still lives in the same old hut.'

'That's a beautiful story you've told me,' the king said, bowing his head.

The minister stood in silence before the king. After a moment or two the king continued. 'Was this the silver mountain you had in mind when you told me that the minister here could find me all the money I need?'

'Yes,' the other responded.

'Well, I can't put the thumbscrews on him,' the king said, 'and how else would I get a man like that to show me the mountain? A man who has denied himself both his beloved and all the wealth in the world.'

'That's a different matter,' the minister said. 'But if his native country were to be in need of treasure, I've no doubt he might come round to it.'

'Will you vouch for that?' the king asked.

'Yes, I'll vouch for it,' the minister said.

'And he won't be concerned about how his parishioners take it?'

'That can be left in the hands of God.'

The king rose from his chair and walked over to the window. He stood for a while, looking out at the crowd of people. The longer he looked, the brighter his big eyes shone and his whole figure seemed to grow.

'You can tell the minister of this parish,' the king said, 'that there is no finer sight for the King of Sweden than to see people like these people.'

Then the king turned away from the window, looked at the minister and began to smile. 'Could it be that the minister of this parish is so poor that he takes off his black vestments and dresses like a farmer the moment the service is over?' the king asked.

'Yes, he is that poor,' the minister said, his coarse face suddenly blushing.

The king went back to the window. It was obvious he was in the very best of spirits. Everything noble and grand within him had been wakened to life. 'You shall leave the mine undisturbed,' the king said. 'Since you've gone hungry and toiled your whole life to make these people the way you want them to be, you may keep things as they are.'

'And if the kingdom is in danger?' the minister said.

'The kingdom is better served with people than with money,' the king said. And having said this, he bade the minister farewell and left the vestry.

The crowd outside was standing there as silent and taciturn as when he'd gone in. But when the king came out, a farmer approached him.

'Have you had a chance to speak to our minister?' the farmer asked.

'Yes,' said the king, 'I've spoken to him.'

'In that case you will have been given our answer?' the farmer said. 'We told you to go in and talk to our minister and he would give our answer.'

'Yes,' the king said, 'I have been given the answer.'

(From *En saga om en saga och andra sagor*, 1908.)

Notes

126 *Gustav III*: Gustav III (1746-92) came to the throne in 1771 and was assassinated in 1792. A believer in enlightened absolutism, he seized power from the Riksdag and the estates in a coup in 1772, thus ending the period known as the Age of Liberty during which power had alternated between the Hat Party (mainly upper aristocracy) and the Cap Party (mainly lower aristocracy). He introduced many progressive economic, penal and social reforms and suppressed endemic corruption. Gustav was a great and uniquely generous patron of the arts: the Royal Opera, the Royal Theatre and the Swedish Academy

were all founded during his reign.

127 *the perilous state in which the kingdom found itself*: Gustav went to war against Russia in 1788 in a failed attempt to re-establish the Swedish Baltic possessions lost in the Great Northern War (1700-21). This led to unrest and conspiracy among the officer corps, particularly in Swedish Finland. Taking advantage of this, Denmark invaded. In 1790 peace was made with Russia and the Danes persuaded to make peace. Meanwhile dissatisfaction with the king was growing among the aristocracy, though he remained popular with the common people. He was assassinated by the Swedish officer J.J. Anckarström at a masked ball in 1792. (Verdi's opera *Un ballo in maschera*, 1859, is loosely based on the assassination.)

132 *Falun*: a town in Dalarna,140 miles north of Stockholm and now a World Heritage Site. Falun (population 37,000) is the oldest industrial area in Sweden, centred on the enormous copper mine, which was chartered as early as 1347 though there is evidence of copper mining many centuries earlier than that. In 1646 Queen Kristina is reputed to have said 'The greatness of the realm stands and falls with the copper mountain'. The characteristic red colour of Swedish timber cottages is because of a wood-preserving stain that is a by-product of the copper.

135 *soldiers' croft*: a system used in Sweden to organise and finance a trained standing army (Sw. *indelningsverket*, Eng. allotment system). Groups of four farms had to join forces to provide farmland (a croft) and equipment for one soldier. The system functioned from the 1640s until 1901. Soldiers enlisted in this system would take military sounding surnames: in this case, Swedish 'Svärd' is English 'Sword'.

THE SACRED IMAGE IN LUCCA

Den heliga bilden i Lucca*

Translated by Sarah Death

Long ago in the world, it happened that a poor agricultural labourer and his wife came walking down the main street in Palermo. The woman led a donkey loaded with two baskets of vegetables and the man followed behind with a goad to drive the beast along. As they proceeded on their way, they caught sight of a monk who was preaching on a street corner. He had attracted a large number of people and the two of them could hear repeated bursts of laughter from the crowd.

'Dear husband,' said the wife, 'if you agree, let us stop here for a few moments and listen to that man of God. He seems to be something of a joker and I would not mind ending the day with a good laugh.'

'In truth, I feel the same,' said the man. 'Our work is done for the day, after all. Why should we deny ourselves a little amusement, particularly when it costs nothing?'

They pushed their way into the crowd, but when they got close enough to be able to see the speaker's expression, they were astonished. He was certainly no clown, as they had first thought, but was delivering his words with the most solemn countenance, although this did not stop his listeners positively squirming with laughter.

'How on earth can this be?' asked the old woman. 'I mean, that monk looks so devout. Why is everyone laughing at him?'

One of the bystanders had heard the old wife's question.

'Don't be surprised to see us laughing,' he said. 'That monk is from Lucca in Italy, and he is begging for money for a sacred image that they say is in a church in that city. He insists this image is so powerful that every gift He is given will be repaid a hundredfold. Can you imagine anything more ridiculous?'

'I am only an uneducated farm labourer,' the old man whispered to his wife. 'I suppose that's why I can't fathom why he finds that so ridiculous.'

They squeezed their way even closer, and finally they could hear the monk with their own ears, affirming that if anyone were willing to make a gift, great or small, to the sacred image of Christ crucified that was kept in the cathedral in Lucca, then they would be repaid a hundred times over.

The monk gave his assurances that he was speaking on the best authority, but the townspeople could not grasp that this was no jest. With every word that he uttered, the gales of laughter grew louder and the ridicule more open.

'I simply can't understand the people of this town,' said the poor woman. 'Don't they realise what a splendid offer this is? I only wish I owned something that I could give to the image.'

'You're quite right,' agreed the man. 'Look at the monk! There's an honest and trustworthy man, who knows what he is talking about. If I were one of the rich townsfolk, I wouldn't hesitate to give my whole fortune to the image so it would be repaid to me a hundred times over.'

'My dear, dear husband,' the woman exclaimed, 'turn your words into deeds! After all, we are not entirely destitute. Don't we have our vegetable patch and our little house and our old donkey? We would not raise a very large sum if we sold them, but just think of it instantly growing a hundredfold. We would surely be so wealthy that we would have bread until our dying days.'

'You take the words right out of my mouth,' replied her husband. 'We have struggled and laboured all our lives and never grown any richer despite our efforts. Now the time is approaching when we will no longer be able to provide for ourselves. We should not miss a chance like this to ensure ourselves an old age free from cares.'

With that, their minds were made up. The next day they sought out their neighbour, a farmer who was both prosperous and wise, and asked him if he would buy their house, their garden and their old donkey.

The rich farmer had long coveted the little patch of ground adjacent to his own farm and was gratified to get the offer. But before completing the purchase he was anxious, as any good neighbour should be, to establish what the old folk planned to live on, once they had sold their property, and that almost put an end to the whole business.

'It is true enough,' he exclaimed when he heard how they intended to invest their money, 'that I have long wished to have your garden in my possession, so I could put a road across the land, but I simply cannot be held responsible for granting your wish, when I hear that you intend to use the proceeds of the sale in such a foolish way. You have been my neighbours for over thirty years, and I want no part in your downfall.'

The two old people again explained to him that they had heard a monk say that the sacred image had the power to repay them a hundred times over.

'So why not a thousand times over, for that matter?' said the neighbour. 'That is the sort of thing monks say as a matter of course, never expecting anyone to take them seriously.'

The farmer made all the objections that an honest man should in such a case. It was only when the old couple threatened to offer their property to someone else who lived nearby that he relented. He bought the whole lot from them for a sum of thirty florins, which he counted out from a leather pouch. 'There!' he said. 'There is the money, but do not come back here and complain to me when it is all gone and you have no recourse but to go begging.'

'Dear neighbour,' said the old woman, 'when you next see us, we will own a hundred times as many florins as we do today. Why, then, should we trouble you or anybody else by begging for alms?'

'Well,' said the farmer, and laughed, 'the pair of you are so crazed that there is no point in reasoning with you. Just tell me what you are going to do first of all.'

'What we are going to do!' echoed the poor man. 'Neighbour, what else would we do but make our way to Lucca with our gift and lay it at the feet of the sacred image?'

'My word, that monk must have been a wizard to skew your minds like that,' the farmer declared with some vehemence. 'How can you imagine that the effigy of a saint can pay out a precise sum like that? Or why you two should be helped in such a miraculous way, above and beyond everybody else? I have a daughter who has been sick and bedridden for over a year. If you knew what offerings I have made to Santa Rosalia of Palermo and other saints! But do you think I have received any aid? No, I tell you that not one of those holy images has lifted a finger for her sake. She will die soon, I am certain, and that will put an end to all the joy in my life.'

Once the rich man had uttered these words, he waved goodbye to his neighbours and retreated swiftly into his house, for he was close to tears.

The poor couple stood there for a moment and watched him go. 'It is a simple truth that no one is spared sorrow,' said the wife, dabbing her eyes. 'Be sure to remember, dear husband, that we must pray to the sacred image and ask for our dear neighbour to be enlightened as to why his prayers are not heard! He is a good man, who surely deserves to have his favourite child still alive.'

The old couple then went to bid a fond farewell to their loyal donkey, and after that there was nothing to keep them in their home district and they could set forth on their journey to Lucca.

They did not want to eat into their sum of thirty florins, however, so they had to walk all the way and were reduced to begging for their food and overnight lodgings. It was thus no easy journey, but despite this they were able to cover the distances without any real difficulty, until they reached Messina, where they were in need of a ferry to get across the strait that separates Sicily from the mainland. When they came down to the harbour, they soon spied a small ferryboat, intended for those who were travelling on foot, without too much baggage. They were about to step aboard when they were turned back by the ferryman, a poor galley slave who was fettered to his vessel by strong chains.

'No, no, my fellow Christians,' he said. 'Neither of you boards this ferry until you have each paid half a florin for the crossing.'

He had stretched out as best he could on the rowing seat and gave the pious wanderers a rather hostile glare, for they had reached the ferry in the worst of the midday heat, when all activity ceased and he had the right to a couple of hours' rest.

'My friend,' replied the poor man, 'I realise that you take us for beggars, who want to make use of your labour and give you nothing for it, but that is not at all the case. On the contrary, we are making our way to Italy to invest our money at interest and when we come back, we will most likely be so rich that we can pay you five florins, if you so wish. Help us across the strait for nothing this time and you will not have cause to regret it.'

The galley slave raised his head slightly, squinted at them through half-closed eyes and settled back once more.

'Oh yes, you look just the sort of people who would have money to invest,' he said.

'As I live and breathe,' said the poor man, 'I have no less than thirty florins in my bag, but I do not want to touch them, because they are intended for someone who repays all that he is given a hundredfold. So you can understand that I do not want to spend any of that sum now, but would rather pay you when I come back.'

The ferryman raised his head again, with slightly greater interest.

'And what manner of person is it, who repays a hundred times over?' he said.

'Who could it be but the sacred image in Lucca?' exclaimed the poor man.

The galley slave burst into bitter laughter.

'Let me tell you something,' he said. 'It is true that I have orders from the authorities to demand half a florin from every person I ferry across the strait, but in my free time, like now, I have the right to take you across for nothing. Do not thank me for it, for it would be much more merciful not to carry you any further, but I have no inclination to be merciful, and that is why

I shall take you to Italy. Once you are there, you may perhaps find your way to Lucca, and there you will see that you have been duped.'

He nodded to them to step into the boat. He said nothing at all in the course of the crossing, but when they put in at Reggio in Italy, he resumed his bitter tirade.

'As you are so certain that this image will help you, I want to tell you that no one can have sent up as many prayers as I have, sitting here chained to these oars as I am. I should also have received help, for I am not held here on account of any crime I have committed, but as a result of an unjust verdict. It should be the task of the great powers in Heaven to set such cases right, but I detect no sign that a single one of them has cared to do anything for me.'

When the poor couple had clambered out of the boat and were on their way up the beach, the old woman remarked that the world was richer in sorrow and misfortune then she had ever thought.

'Too true,' said the man. 'The distressed are everywhere. Keep it in mind, dear wife, that we must not forget to ask the almighty image why this man cannot have his prayers heard and be set free from his suffering!'

After that they continued on their way, and headed northwards, a walk that took them many weeks and months. One evening they finally reached a city that people told them was Lucca.

'Dear husband,' said the old woman as they entered through the city gates, 'how happy I am that we have reached our journey's end! If you feel the same way, let us go to the duomo right away. I want neither to eat nor to rest until I have seen the sacred image.'

'You are quite right,' said the husband, 'but if we are to have time to present our gift to the image today, we must hurry. It is so late in the day that it cannot be long before evening prayer is over in the churches and their great doors are shut.'

Although they were tired after a full day's walking they quickened their steps and when they were within sight of the outer walls of the duomo, they broke into a run. But they were too late. The sacristan, who looked after the sacred building, stood on the front steps tucking the heavy keyring back onto his belt as they approached.

'Oh Sacristan, dear Sacristan,' began the old woman, who happened to get there first. 'Won't you have pity on us and let us into the church, just for a few moments? You don't know how far we have walked to get here. We have come all the way from Palermo to give a gift to the sacred image that is kept here.'

'Gentle Sacristan!' cried the old man, interrupting his wife, 'we are not beggars. Here is a pouch containing thirty florins that we intend to give to your miracle-working image, because we know He will pay us back a hundredfold.'

They were so eager that they grabbed hold of the sacristan's cowl to keep him there. But their fervour made the guardian of the duomo begin to think them both deranged.

'What is wrong with you people?' he exclaimed. 'The church is closed for today. There will be no mass until tomorrow morning.'

'Dear friend,' said the woman, 'we do not want to hear mass. We have priests and churches enough in Sicily and we have not come all this long way for that. The one and only reason we have come is to give thirty florins to your sacred image because we know that He repays all the gifts He receives a hundred times over.'

The poor woman spoke with even greater conviction than usual because she had now come to a place where she felt certain to be understood. But the sacristan was as taken aback by her declaration as everyone else.

'Dear Sacristan,' said the woman, 'you must surely know that this is the way things are. It was a monk from this city who told us about the image, down in Palermo.'

'I assure you, my friends, that I am ignorant of this,' said the sacristan, 'and that I do not comprehend a word of what you are saying. It would be as well for the two of you to tell me everything you know of the matter. You look like shrewd and sensible people, but you speak as if you were out of your minds.'

As they told their story from the very beginning, the cathedral guardian thought:

'If these people are so persistent that they have walked all the way from Palermo to Lucca to give money to the sacred image, then there is no point in refusing them entry to the church. They will not settle for anything less than my opening the door for them.'

And he actually took the bunch of keys from his belt and prepared to unlock the door, even as he made one last attempt to talk them out of their delusion. 'Alas, my friends,' he said as he wrestled with the stiff locks, 'admittedly it is true that there is an old image of Christ on the cross here in the church, but it is in a sorry state. It hangs unnoticed on a pillar, and no one who comes here addresses their prayers to it. I swear that in the twenty-five years I have been the cathedral sacristan, it has not performed a single miracle.'

The two old folk were extremely surprised by what they had just been told.

'Ah, my friends,' the sacristan went on, 'if the image had the power that you ascribe to Him, then He should at least be able to help the rosebush that grows here against the church wall. It was my greatest joy in times gone by to see it in bloom. It covered this whole corner with the most beautiful roses climbing way up the tower, but a few years ago it stopped flowering. I water it and tend it as best I can, and it certainly looks green and healthy. I simply cannot understand why I am no longer granted the pleasure of seeing its fair array.'

He gave a deep sigh and looked so genuinely distressed that the two poor wanderers declared that as soon as they stood before the sacred image, they would ask why the rose bush no longer produced any flowers, but he appeared to pay no heed to their promises.

'You hurry now,' he said, as he pushed open the door of the church, 'and I will stay out here and wait for you. It is not difficult to find the image, for it is hanging on the pillar closest to the lighted lamp.'

The old couple had been nonplussed by his explanations, it is true, but their faith was not shaken in the slightest, and the moment they saw that the door was open, they rushed into the church. Once inside, however, they stopped short, for in that ancient house of God which had few small windows, like narrow slits, it was already completely dark. At the very front there was indeed a small red flame burning but they did not know how they would find their way to it without bumping into pillars and tombs.

The old woman took one pace forward but almost tripped down a step and halted in alarm.

'Dear husband,' she said, 'what ill luck for us. Knowing that the sacred image is just a few steps away yet not being able to reach it!'

'Keep still for a few minutes, until our eyes grow used to the darkness in here!' whispered her husband. He was far too infused with the holiness of the place to dare speak out loud.

All at once the little red flame burning at the front of the church seemed to them to divide itself in two. One half began to float back and forth around the church, and as it went from place to place, the candles on the altar and in the chandeliers were suddenly lit and the darkness instantly dispersed.

'Oh, my dear husband,' said the old woman, 'can you see them lighting candles down there at the front? Soon it will be easy for us to find the sacred image.'

'Dear wife,' said the man, 'the sacristan was more kindly disposed than we imagined. He has come in through the sacristy to light some candles so that we can find our way.'

'But I can't understand him going to such lengths for our sake. Two or three candles would have been enough, yet as you can see he is not just lighting candles on the high altar but also in the side chapels and the chandeliers.'

It really was true. The whole duomo was shimmering in the candlelight. But at that moment the poor couple were so engrossed in thoughts of the miraculous image that they were no longer curious about the great number of candle flames or how they had been lit.

'Perhaps there is going to be a saint's festival here,' said the old woman. 'In any case, I am glad the candles have been lit. I always feel twice as solemn, when I see so many lighted candles in a church. Do you know what? I would really like it if the organ was playing as well.'

149

The words were barely out of her mouth before a faint swell of notes could be heard from the organ loft.

'Well, listen to that!' said the man. 'I do believe you are to have everything you ask for this evening. And how beautifully they play in this church! I have never heard such glorious music even in the duomo in Palermo.'

'It is so lovely that one might think it was an angel playing,' said the old woman, 'but I expected nothing less in this church. Now my only wish is that it was filled with incense too, because scented clouds of incense always make me feel I am in a sacred place.'

The wife had hardly finished speaking before the old man exclaimed with astonishment in his voice: 'Have you ever caught such a wonderful scent? It is the finest, softest and loveliest incense I have ever known.'

They could not see anyone swinging a censer, any more than they had made out the figure of an organist up in the organ loft, but they tried not to ponder how this had all come about. They lived only for their thoughts of the sacred image. They had now set off towards it, but they walked very slowly up the central aisle because it would have seemed inappropriate to show any haste.

About halfway along the church they had reason to pause when they saw someone walking down the aisle towards them. It was a tall and comely woman wearing a blue dress and a red mantle. She had a little crown of pearls and precious stones on her head and rich ornaments on her arms and at her neck.

She advanced to meet them with the most benevolent of smiles, rather like the lady of the house who is there to greet honoured and eagerly anticipated guests, and she asked them what they were seeking in the church so late at night.

'Most esteemed lady queen,' said the old woman with joy in her voice, for she did not think that she had ever beheld such a beautiful face. 'We have come here, I and my husband, to present our offering to the sacred image of the crucified Christ that is said to hang on a pillar in this church.'

Then the two old people began, as was their wont, to tell their whole story, from that evening when they had heard the monk preaching in the main street of Palermo all the way through to their encounter with the sacristan, outside on the church steps.

The stranger continued to regard them as kindly as before but it seemed to them that her face assumed a more sorrowful expression as their story unfolded.

'Alas,' she said when she had heard them out, 'it is not for me to say whether your hopes will be fulfilled, but I fear the worst. There is nothing so rare as God being in a position to grant people's wishes. Their torment might have been visited on them as a punishment for some misdeed.'

'Look, for example, at the sacristan waiting outside,' she went on. 'He complains that a rosebush of which he is very fond no longer flowers, but it does not occur to him that this is meant as a reminder specifically to him. For a number of years, he has allowed the many images of saints that you see around you to fall into total neglect, not troubling himself to maintain the gilding on their crowns or to repair the damage that they so readily suffer in the course of all those processions. He finds it hard that God does not help him to experience the joy that he desires but first he has to understand that if he is going to ask God to adorn the rose tree with roses, he must not neglect to ensure that the images of these holy men and women of God entrusted to his care can be seen in all their splendour and glory.'

'Ah yes,' said the old couple with a sigh. 'We thought it must be something like that. We have no doubt sinned more gravely than he has, but we came here trusting to the promise that has been given us.'

The beautiful woman before them raised her eyebrows slightly but then went on in the same gentle voice.

'Strong faith is a good thing, but it cannot be sufficient in itself for God to hear your prayers. You could easily ask for something that would actually cause you harm.

'You told me just now about the wretched galley slave at the oars of a ferryboat between Messina and Reggio,' she went on. 'Only a few years ago he was a rich merchant, and furthermore he was a good man, who would not hurt a soul, but he was so addicted to a life of luxury and the pleasures of the flesh that he would have brought terrible sicknesses upon himself and would very likely have died a long time ago, if God had not visited misfortune upon him. It so happened that a thief stole a crown bedecked with gemstones from an image of the Virgin Mary in the duomo, and to deflect suspicion the thief wrenched one of the jewels off the crown and slipped it into the merchant's pocket. The gemstone was found on him, he was immediately accused of having stolen the Madonna's crown, and despite all his avowals of innocence he was sentenced to be chained fast to the ferry and to transport travellers across the strait for the rest of his life. Nothing would have been easier than to help him, for the thief had hidden the crown in a corner of the church attic and left it there. The moment it came to light, it would provide proof of the merchant's innocence and he would be released, but how can God allow that, before the man has changed his disposition? If he received help too soon, he would instantly throw himself back into his former way of life and be assured of his own destruction.'

'Dear and gracious lady!' said the old man, 'we are glad that this is why this man has to suffer the consequences of an unjust verdict. We ourselves thought that this must be the way of it. As for us, we have no idea whether what we wish for will benefit or harm us; we have only that promise in which to place our trust.'

Once more the fair vision before them raised an eyebrow, as if in impatience at their stubbornness, and then continued in a voice that sounded ever gentler, the longer she spoke.

'There is much to be said for a strong faith, but it is still no guarantee that God will hear your prayers. It could be that He first wants to teach you to be content with the good things that have already been allotted to you.

'Here I am thinking of your neighbour, the rich farmer on the edge of Palermo,' she went on. 'Besides the daughter who is ill and bedridden he has another, but she is very plain and slightly deformed, and for that reason her father has always treated her less well. But she is wise and good and hard-working and renders him great service. Her suffering has moved God, so he has sent her sister a sickness, and although it could easily be cured because it was caused only by a poisoned comb that a wicked Arab woman sold her, she still might have to die of it if her father cannot learn to love both his children equally. The sick girl could simply stop combing her hair with the harmful comb and she would gradually recover, but that will not happen until her father has learned the true value of the good gift that God has given him in his less attractive daughter.'

'Oh yes!' declared the old woman. 'The longer I hear you speak, gracious lady, the more convinced I am of God's wisdom and justice. We have most certainly often failed to thank Him for all his blessings, but even so we put our trust in the promise that has been given to us.'

At these words the loveliest smile lent radiance to the noble lady's face as she gestured to the poor couple to follow her, but she said:

'I have warned you, my friends, but I can see that it is impossible to make you abandon your intentions. Yet before you part with your florins, consider once more how hard it is to have your prayers answered!'

Not waiting for an answer, she took them to a pillar and pointed upwards. There, right up by the roof, hung a big cross of darkened wood, and fixed to it was an image of Christ that was so unlike all the other crucifixion images the poor people had ever beheld that they turned to their companion to ask if they were in the right spot.

'This image is very old,' she said, 'and very badly preserved, but it does indeed portray my son, the crucified Redeemer.'

The two old people were so engrossed in looking at the sacred image that they did not at once take in her words, but only understood the full implication of them later.

'Dear husband,' whispered the old woman, 'the holy image up there almost frightens me with His thick eyebrows and deep-set eyes. It makes me anxious to see Him depicted without a beard. I don't recognise him.'

They were also surprised that the image was dressed in a short tunic of some black fabric and had a belt around its waist and wooden sandals on its feet. Moreover, it was very dusty and had clearly been hanging there for years without anyone thinking to attend to it.

'You no doubt feel very uneasy,' said their companion. 'You were expecting the Almighty One who would render you His aid to look quite different.'

'Dear, gracious lady queen,' said the old man, 'we are thinking nothing of the kind. We are glad that we did not immediately recognise Him. We know that the same thing happened when He was here on Earth, that He was humble in outward appearance and that people did not at once realise He was the Son of God.'

The smile reappeared in all its brightness on the unknown woman's face.

'Then present your gift to Him!' she said.

Without a further word the two old people sank to their knees and bowed their heads low to the stone floor.

'O Christ, Son of God,' they said, 'receive our gift, and hear our prayer! Here are the thirty florins we made when we sold our garden, our house and our old donkey! We have brought them here all the way from Sicily because we know that You repay a hundredfold each gift that You are offered. Do not let our faith have been in vain, but give us as much as will permit us to enjoy an old age free from care!'

As they were saying this, the man untied the bag of florins from his belt and pushed it over to the pillar supporting the cross.

They uttered the same words over again without raising their heads, but suddenly they heard a slight creaking from above. They raised their eyes and saw that the wooden image had freed one arm and one foot from the nails that were driven through them.

The old woman gripped her husband's hand hard but neither of them spoke. Their hearts were pounding with blissful expectation. They felt more certain than ever that their prayers would be answered.

But in one rapid movement the image of Christ loosened the sandal from his foot and let it drop to the two supplicants. Then He resumed his normal position and looked down at them from His cross with the same stern and sorrowful expression as before.

All this was the work of a moment, and they could easily have thought their eyes had deceived them, had the sandal not been there on the floor in front of them.

It was a very ordinary sandal with a wooden sole and leather straps. It had neither jewels nor ornaments but was entirely worthless. It was as if the noble lady, who was still standing there beside them, could sense that the poor couple felt cheated of their expectations.

'Alas,' she said sympathetically. 'This sandal is poor recompense for your great gift. But it is still not too late to change your minds. You can just leave it lying there and take back your florins.'

The look that the two old folk gave her was almost like chastisement.

'What do you mean, dear and gracious lady?' they said. 'The sacred image has most certainly given us as much as He could in His poverty. He has performed a miracle so He could present us with this sandal. This is assuredly worth a thousand times more than our poor florins.'

Hardly had they said this than the exalted lady's face lit up in the tenderest of smiles.

'You are my son's rightful servants,' she said. 'And you shall not be deceived in your trust in Him. God can always grant the innocent wishes of the devout.'

As she said this, a halo of such brightness and lustre shone around her that the old couple had to close their eyes. When they opened them again, the church was in darkness, the candles were extinguished, the organ music had stopped and the radiant female figure that had so recently stood before them was gone.

But they barely had time to wonder about the transformation. They were not alone for so much as a second. The church door flew open and the sacristan came rushing in.

'Dear, holy pilgrims,' he cried, 'what a miracle!* I saw it. I sat on the steps waiting for you, but time went by and still you did not come, so I got up and looked through the keyhole. I saw you advance amid beams of celestial light, and God's Holy Mother, who is normally enthroned on an altar here at the front, had stepped down and was walking by your side. Then I saw the crucified Christ lean over you to give you the gift of His sandal. Oh, you must come with me to his lordship the bishop right away!'

He took them to the bishop, who was seated in the chapter-house, surrounded by his dean and canons.

He gave his account. The two old people gave theirs, and at length the pious gentlemen understood what a great miracle had occurred.

The very first thing the bishop did was to call his treasurer to him.

'My friend,' he said, 'I wish to purchase the sandal, which these good people have received from the sacred image in such a miraculous way, for 3,000 florins, if they will sell it to me. I do not want it to be lost to Lucca.'

Once the money had been counted out and placed in the old man's hand, the bishop continued:

'Before you leave Lucca, I invite you to join us all to see the sacred image moved into its rightful place above the high altar, but then you must make haste to return home the same way as you came, and be sure to give anyone who will listen an account of everything you have experienced along the way. It gratifies me to know that, through you, the galley slave will be liberated from his oar and your good neighbour's daughter will be cured of her sickness, just as I am sure that the sacristan will not neglect to allow the cathedral rose tree to come into full bloom.'

He fell silent for a moment and then extended his hands over the two old people.

'You are wise, and the rest of us are fools,' he said. 'We too know that God is all-powerful, but which of us dares trust to His succour? Thank God for giving you the gift of faith! It is the greatest of His blessings.'

(From *Troll och Människor*, 1915.)

Notes

141 *Den heliga bilden i Lucca*: Lagerlöf wrote many *legender*, stories of the lives of saints, several of them linked to individual

Italian cities that she and her friend Sophie Elkan visited on their travels in 1895-96. 'The Sacred Image in Lucca' was one of these; it was the last of her *legender*, not written until 1913. Historians and art historians do not agree on the reliability of sources describing how *Il volto santo*, (literally, 'the sacred face') came to be brought to Lucca, possibly from the Holy Land. Lagerlöf was unlikely to have been aware of these scholarly disputes but she saw the image on her visit to Lucca and was impressed by its penetrating gaze. *Il volto santo* is in fact a crucifix, most likely the work of the Lombardian sculptor Benedetto Antelami in the twelfth or thirteenth century. Lagerlöf's own version of the story was probably inspired in part by a book she is known to have owned, a collection of Sicilian folk tales including 'Lu signuri di Luca', published in 1888 by Guiseppe Pitré, a professor of folk psychology at the University of Palermo. Margherita Giordano Lokrantz makes a close study of Lagerlöf and her Lucca story in *Italien och Norden. Kulturförbindelser under ett sekel* (Carlsson bokförlag, 2001), chapters XII and XIII.

For more on Lagerlöf's representations of Italy in her legends see also Elettra Carbone's article '"The Italian Factor": Representations of Italy in Selma Lagerlöf's Legends and Hans Ernst Kinck's Novellas' (*Scandinavica*, 52: 2, 2018).

155 *a miracle!*: As Bjarne Thorup Thomsen writes in the introduction to this volume, when Lagerlöf designates one of her stories a *legend*, this generally signals that its denouement will involve a miracle.

THE MIST

Dimman

Translated by Linda Schenck

June 1916

One autumn morning in 1914 during the first year of the Great War*, quite a heavy mist spread across the small area, peaceful and virtually untainted by world events, where The Peaceable Man had his home. The mist was not so heavy as to prevent him from seeing his entire garden and all his outbuildings, but his gaze could penetrate no further. He could not see either fields or hills or woods. All the usual surroundings had vanished. He could have imagined he was living on a solitary little islet somewhere far off in the seven seas.

He was unaccustomed to having such a short span of sight, so unaccustomed that it brought a painful pressure to his eyes. There was something dispiriting about not having a free view in all directions, and when he took his habitual morning turn around the garden he found himself anxious and worried, as if there were some imminent danger.

Of necessity, his eyebrows furrowed as if trying to force his eyes to focus more sharply so they could penetrate the wall of mist. Nothing of this sort did any good, however, and he had to be satisfied with looking at the things in his immediate surroundings. Rather reluctantly he initially sought distraction in admiring the bright red rowan leaves which the moisture had endowed with a sheen reminiscent of old copper pots. Then his attention moved on to the dewy spiderwebs stretching across a strawberry bed full of languishing plants. He told himself these webs made a lovely autumnal veil, and wondered whether they had given elderly women in times gone by the idea of concealing their fading beauty behind veils decorated with pearls.

He found this thought amusing. His gloom vanished and he gazed around with renewed interest. He was standing in front of an old astrachan tree laden with apples, and the great beauty of this tree took him completely by surprise. Usually, as he walked through his garden, he found this tree annoyingly ugly. It was low and had a broad trunk with thick branches sticking straight out. But at this time of year, when the apples were ripe and the old branches heavy with fruit, they bent in elegant arcs, indicative of both strength and agility. He could see that what appeared to be its lack of grace was necessary to the tree if these branches were to bear the burden that presently weighed them down.

Suddenly he found himself completely reconciled to the mist. It narrowed his viewpoint, forcing him to focus his attention on little things he had previously neglected to enjoy. 'In order to see well and to comprehend what one sees,' he thought to himself. 'it has always been necessary to focus on what is close at hand.'

This understanding was further confirmed as he moved along and discovered a number of ripe green plums, the last ones for the year, which had hitherto evaded all prying eyes. The mist seemed to have altered his sense of sight, and he quickly harvested the shiny little plums. Suddenly he became aware, for the first time that morning, of a sound from elsewhere in the world. A deep, powerful voice shouted from within the mist:

'Dear Lord, have mercy and help the combatants! Please, please please, take pity on the combatants!'

He stopped to listen. The words were clearly audible from out of the mist, but there was no human being in sight.

'Dear Lord, have mercy and help the combatants! Please, please please, take pity on the combatants, who are in such dire straits. Blood flows like water in the trenches. Please, please please dear Lord.'

The Peaceable Man, who had been walking along deep in

calm and pleasant thought, gestured impatiently. Not the war again! Not for a single moment was anyone spared. If you turned your thoughts elsewhere, nature seemed to develop a voice of its own to bring you back to awareness of the horror that was enveloping mankind.

Again there was a call from within the mist:

'Blood is flowing like water in the trenches. The fields are piled high as haystacks with corpses. Please, please please help the combatants!'

Of course it had to be that madwoman who was always wandering the area praying and singing, who had now begun calling out to God to take pity on the soldiers of the great powers. She was probably up on the road that ran along the edge of the woods, invisible now in the mist. It touched him to hear her, although at the same time he found it difficult to suppress a smile thinking of the poor creature who wished to construct a dam of her prayers that would hold back the world war.

'Help the combatants so there will be peace for them!' the madwoman repeated. 'Blood is flowing like water in the trenches…'

He stood still, listening until her voice was no longer heard. Then he sighed and walked on.

Indeed, these were such times as could make anyone take to the roads and byways shouting their anxiety.

The Peaceable Man groaned at the thought of this struggle that now impacted virtually every human being and threatened the destruction of the entire world. If only what they were experiencing had been a storm surge or an erupting volcano! Their misfortune would have been no less, but they would not have to have the humiliating sense that humanity was at fault and that they had brought this upon themselves. Nor would they have to think that because they were rational human beings who had been seized by the insanity of war there ought to be a word to be said or a measure to be taken to bring this frenzy to an end. They would not have to spend every hour of every day in pain and anxiety, worrying their heads in search of a dam to hold back the destruction.

'What can I do?' he asked himself. 'My words would not

have any greater impact than those of that miserable, troubled woman walking around out there. And yet…'

He could not shake off the feeling that he ought to be doing something, and not just sitting still.

On his walk he had now reached the far corner of the garden and, as he turned back, the picture that opened before him was a cheerful and captivating one.

From where The Peaceable Man stood he could see a gentle upward slope toward his home. He viewed the entirety of his old farm with its red buildings and all the brightly colored autumnal foliage. This was more or less what he saw every single day, but the whole place looked different because the mist had singled it out from its ordinary surroundings.

Now that he saw his farm in isolation, he noticed for the first time how prettily his red home up on the hillock blended in with the green and yellow treetops around it, with the smaller outbuildings, with the billowing vegetation below it and the low circle of newly planted fruit trees encircling the bottom of the hill. Never had it all come together in such harmony as today, framed by the mist filling all the interstices. Nothing could be removed; it all had to remain, each thing in its given place. Brought together by the mist and the greenery, his home became more appealing than ever before. It radiated security and comfort. He felt calm and joyous at the very sight of it.

All of a sudden, he had a remarkable flash. He conceived of himself as alone with his farm. He imagined himself and the farm having a quiet life, undisturbed, surrounded by the mist which acted as a wall, concealing them from the world. It would guard them, day after day, so thick and impenetrable that not even passersby in coaches up on the road by the woods would know they were there, close by.

The postman with his black satchel would not find his way to the farm in the deceptive mist. No visitors, no strangers would be able to find the beginning of the lane leading up to the farmhouse. Nothing from the outside world would find its way to the farm, nor would anything from the farm find its way to the outside world.

Winter would follow autumn, summer would follow spring

in slow succession. Snow would fall and melt, the earth and the trees would be clad in greenery and the greenery would fade and disappear. Cold and heat would alternate in finding their way there, but the hazy mist would simply remain throughout.

They, he and his farm, would be living a dream life. One chore would follow the next. Harvest would follow sowing, and baking would follow brewing in slow alternation. Cows would be milked, sheep sheared, yarn spun, tablecloths of shiny damask appear as if by magic in the loom. They would have to live by the sweat of their own brows. Nothing would be brought in, and nothing removed. The sorrow that weighed them down would be their own. They would have no one to depend on but one another. They would be living on an island in the seven seas, to which no vessels could find their way.

What gave The Peaceable Man the greatest pleasure of all was the anticipation of escaping the horrors of the Great War. He opened his arms to the mist and spoke:

'Stay, oh mist, stay! We are moving toward terrible times. Let me be spared from living through them! Safeguard my farm with your white walls! Let me live here on my ancestral land without having to be aware of the violence and bloodshed! Let me and my people remain here, quietly performing our labors without interruption from the rumors of the misfortunes of strangers.

'Birds will find their way to us now and then, but we will not seek any messages under their wings. On occasional mornings we will hear that poor madwoman pass by with her loud prayers. But we will not extend ourselves to hear whether it is still the combatants she is praying for.

'One day when it is all over, when the battles are finished and people are no longer fighting one another, you will dissolve and vanish. And we, knowing nothing of the horrors that have taken place, we will go out into the world rapturous to celebrate the eternal solemnity of life. Our senses will not have been tainted with tales of violence and bloodshed. Our hearts will not despair from having heard tales of misfortune we were unable to affect. We will return to the world with confidence that human beings are gentle by nature and cherish peaceful reconstruction. We will be like the pious Seven Sleepers, who were spared from violent times to find that it is possible for happiness and peace to return, that misery and hardship are not the only things earth has to offer its unfortunate children.'

After these words, The Peaceable Man heard two separate sounds. A gust of wind blew through the mist, hissing like a serpent. That was one. The other was a soft echo of the prayer of the miserable wandering woman.

'Help the combatants to find peace, O Lord,' it resounded from a long distance. It sounded almost like a warning, but he did not let it stop him.

'Let me walk here in my garden, oh mist,' he shouted, 'let me go on discovering beautiful little things! Teach me to rest my eyes on that which is close at hand! Let me labor in a way that is my own, occupy myself with things I am capable of doing! Let me be spared rushing from one end of the country to another like a mad person trying to solve problems that are far beyond my control!'

After he uttered these words, he once again heard a murmuring in the mist. He seemed to hear something that sounded like 'Your will be done.'

However, this was naturally nothing but self-deception. At almost the same moment, a fresh breeze picked up. It ripped the mist to shreds, tossing it every which way. Everything took on its usual form again, and he smiled softly at the thoughts the mist had awoken in him and which would never be realized. But such wishes are dangerous to make. The powers of nature sometimes take a vicious pleasure in granting our most absurd wishes.

From that day onward The Peaceable Man became aware that although the news of the war only continued to grow more and more horrifying, he was no longer as emotionally upset by it. Everything that happened felt alien and distant, as if it had no bearing on him at all. He just performed his usual chores, unbothered by anxiety over the way the world was being destroyed.

The man, who had no idea it was the mist that had heard his plea and settled lethargically in around his soul, persuaded himself that he had grown more balanced and gained wisdom.

He commended himself on his intelligence and caution. All his desire to find a way of putting a stop to the deluge of evil that had been loosed on the world also sank in the fog which enveloped his good sense without his being aware of it. All his desire for action gave way to bewilderment, but he was so indifferent that he counted himself fortunate for being wise enough to show forbearance, rather than overexerting himself in pointless efforts.

He noted that others, no more prominent than himself, raised their voices to have a say, but he was unable to see that their words had any impact. He considered them not unlike the woman he had heard praying to God that misty autumn morning. He felt that they must be bewildered souls who were meddling in affairs they had neither the power nor the authority to affect.

And yet in the depths of his own soul he followed their doings with terrible anxiety. On beautiful, starry nights the mist lost its influence over him and he worried desperately about the moment when he would have to leave earthly life behind and confront his Maker. And he knew that when the time came he would be standing at the throne of Our Lord next to the woman who had wandered the roads pleading to God. And God the Father would address him severely:

'I unleashed a storm over the world in your time. Where did your heart get the idea that you could hide away from that storm?'

The Peaceable Man thought he would reply in his own defense:

'That which Thou demanded of me was beyond human power to accomplish. I kept my own counsel because I could see no alternative. It was not up to me to subdue Thy storm. I feared that I would do more harm than good.'

And the Great Judge would then reply:

'I know that I never gave you the ability to subdue the storm. But I did give you sufficient power to display compassion and exercise charity.'

The Peaceable Man would then point to the woman standing

beside him before the throne of God.

'This woman has spoken and spoken incessantly,' he would say, 'and what good has it done?'

'This woman's cries have been unable to move hearts of the worldly powers that be,' He who reigns over heaven and earth would answer, 'but her prayers have opened to her both my embrace and the way to the glory of my realm.'

Thus The Peaceable Man would come to know that for him there was no hope, and in his despair he would sink further and further down from the throne of Our Lord into the place where all is cold and dark and silent and petrified in a haze of lethargy.

(From *Troll och människor*, 1915.)

Note

158 *The Great War*: Sweden, like Norway and Denmark, remained neutral in First World War, continuing a policy initiated after the Napoleonic wars. At court, among the aristocracy and the officer class, there was, however, considerable support for Germany.

SELMA LAGERLÖF

The Löwensköld Ring
Charlotte Löwensköld
Anna Svärd

(translated by Linda Schenck)

The Löwensköld Ring (1925) is the first volume of the trilogy considered
to have been Selma Lagerlöf's last work of prose fiction. Set in the
Swedish province of Värmland in the eighteenth century, the narrative
traces the consequences of the theft of General Löwensköld's ring
from his coffin, and develops into a disturbing tale of revenge from
beyond the grave. It is also a tale about decisive women. The narrative
twists and the foregrounding of alternative interpretations confront
the reader with a pervasive sense of ambiguity. *Charlotte Löwensköld*
(1925) is the story of the following generations, a tale of psychological
insight and social commentary, and of the complexities of a mother-son
relationship. How we make our life 'choices' and what evil forces can be
at play around us is beautifully and ironically depicted and comes to a
close in the third volume, *Anna Svärd* (1928).

The Löwensköld Ring
ISBN 9781870041928
(Paperback, 120 pages)

Charlotte Löwensköld
ISBN 9781909408067
(Paperback, 290 pages)

Anna Svärd
ISBN 9781909408289
(Paperback, 330 pages)

SELMA LAGERLÖF

Nils Holgersson's Wonderful Journey through Sweden

(translated by Peter Graves)

Nils Holgersson's Wonderful Journey through Sweden (1906-07) is truly unique. Starting life as a commissioned school reader designed to present the geography of Sweden to nine-year-olds, it quickly won the international fame and popularity it still enjoys over a century later. The story of the naughty boy who climbs on the gander's back and is then carried the length of the country, learning both geography and good behaviour as he goes, has captivated adults and children alike, as well as inspiring film-makers and illustrators. The elegance of the present translation – the first full translation into English – is beautifully complemented by the illustrations specially created for the volume.

Nils Holgersson's Wonderful Journey through Sweden, Volume 1
ISBN 9781870041966
(Paperback, 365 pages)

Nils Holgersson's Wonderful Journey through Sweden, Volume 2
ISBN 9781870041973
(Paperback, 380 pages)

Nils Holgersson's Wonderful Journey through Sweden, The Complete Volume
ISBN 9781870041966
(Hardback, 684 pages)

SELMA LAGERLÖF

The Phantom Carriage

(translated by Peter Graves)

Written in 1912, Selma Lagerlöf's *The Phantom Carriage* is a powerful combination of ghost story and social realism, partly played out among the slums and partly in the transitional sphere between life and death. The vengeful and alcoholic David Holm is led to atonement and salvation by the love of a dying Salvation Army slum sister under the guidance of the driver of the death-cart that gathers in the souls of the dying poor. Inspired by Charles Dickens's *A Christmas Carol*, *The Phantom Carriage* remained one of Lagerlöf's own favourites, and Victor Sjöström's 1920 film version of the story is one of the greatest achievements of the Swedish silent cinema.

The Phantom Carriage
ISBN 9781870041911
(Paperback, 126 pages)

SELMA LAGERLÖF

Mårbacka
Memoirs of a Child (Mårbacka II)

(translated by Sarah Death)

The property of Mårbacka in Värmland was where Selma Lagerlöf grew up, immersed in a tradition of storytelling. Financial difficulties led to the loss of the house, but Lagerlöf was later able to buy it back, rebuild and make it the centre of her world. The book *Mårbacka*, the first part of a trilogy written in 1922-32, can be read as many different things: memoir, fictionalised autobiography, even part of Lagerlöf's myth-making about her own successful career as an author. It is part social and family history, part mischievous satire in the guise of innocent, first-person child narration, part declaration of filial love.

In the second part of her notionally autobiographical trilogy, Lagerlöf broadens the perspective from the farm where she grew up to include the people and places around Lake Fryken in her beloved Värmland county. The personal creation myth which she began in *Mårbacka* continues here with a focus on the self-discipline and imagination needed to fulfil a childhood ambition to become an author. It is hard work that sometimes means taking a stand against convention but also a deeply enriching process in a home steeped in storytelling and books.

Mårbacka
ISBN 9781909408296
(Paperback, 270 pages)

Memoirs of a Child
ISBN9781909408715
(Paperback, 258 pages)

KARIN BOYE

Crisis

(translated by Amanda Doxtater)

Malin Forst is a precocious, devout twenty-year-old woman attending a Stockholm teachers' college in the 1930s. Confounded by a sudden crisis of faith, Malin plunges into a depression and a paralysis of will. Oscillating between poetic prose, social realism, fragments of correspondence, and imagined dialogues between the forces of nature, *Crisis* telescopes Malin's distress out into metaphysical planes and back, as her mind stages struggles between black and white, Dionysian and Apollonian, and with an everyday existence that has become unbearably arduous. And then an intense infatuation with a classmate reorients everything.

Crisis
ISBN 9781909408357
(Paperback, 192 pages)

www.ingramcontent.com/pod-product-compliance
Ingram Content Group UK Ltd.
Pitfield, Milton Keynes, MK11 3LW, UK
UKHW021833170825
461963UK00003B/8

9 781909 408739